AF377955

The implausible destiny of

NSONA

This book was translated from the french version
"Nsona ou l'improbable destinée"(2017)
by the author

Also from the same author
(In French)

Le Prince félon
Les éléphants d'ivoire – Episode 1
(2013)
Le roi maudit
Les éléphants d'ivoire - Episode 2
(2016)
Le message
Les éléphants d'ivoire - Episode 3
(2018)

A.B. KOUBEMBA

The implausible destiny of

NSONA

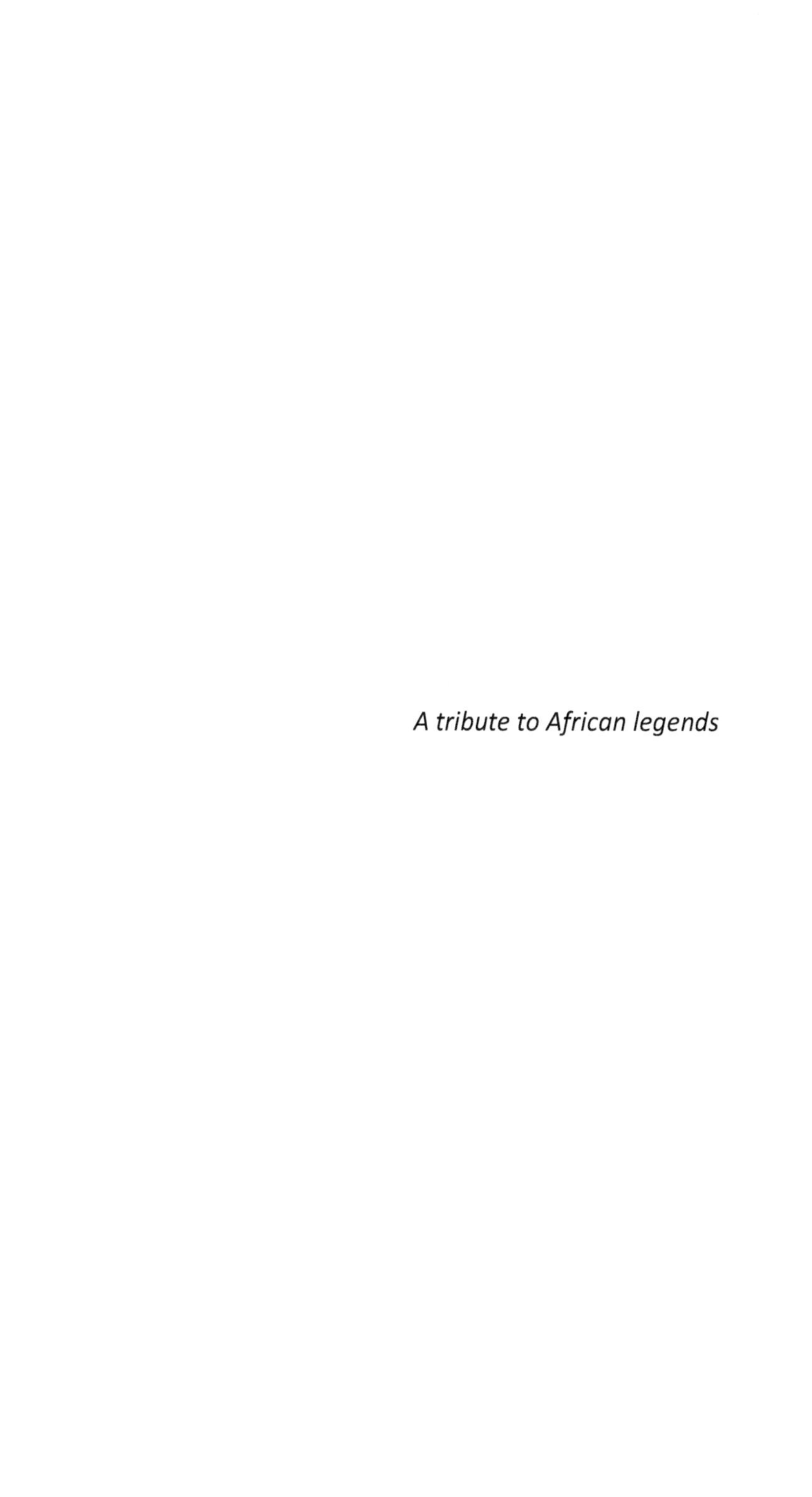

A tribute to African legends

1

"Well, sweetheart! What are you going to purchase from me today?"

The young girl moved forward to the stall, looking somehow embarrassed. She reached out for the fruits that were laid in front of the old woman.

"This is going to be difficult, ma Zinga. I do not have any money on me."

The old woman seemed to be quite chagrined.

"You already told me that yesterday. Do you not ever have any money on you? Cannot I count on you to earn my life?"

The young girl smiled, thus uncovering her beautiful white teeth.

"Oh, please! Do not make me feel guilty; I am sure that many many people appreciate your fruits in this market."

"Greetings to you, ma Zinga! Oh, greetings to you too, Nsona! How are you, both of you?"

"Greetings to you, ma Dienaba! I am fine, what about yourself?"

The young woman and her interlocutor answered at the same time, as if they had prepared a duo. This amused the woman who had just talked to them.

"Well, well, well! What a harmony," she answered. "Thank you I am fine as well."

She moved closer to the fruits on the stall. Her eyes were shining with envy.

"Ma Zinga, I am going to spend some more cowry shells with you today. Your goods are really attractive."

She asked a young boy who was accompanying her to move closer. He presented a cloth bag and she started to put some fruits in it.

"So, you can see now, ma Zinga! What did I just tell you? There will always be someone to buy your goods. If you do not mind, I shall move on!"

Nsona decided to go on her way without even waiting for the answer of the old woman.

She carried on merrily, ignoring the numerous masculine greetings that accompanied her progress. She even behaved in a way to show that she was doing so purposely. She rather paid attention to the many feminine eyes that watched her. Some were envious, others were hostile. But she could not help it, she loved to generate jealousy.

Nsona was a very attractive and exuberant young woman. She not only drew men's and women's eyes on her, but also a lot of husbands who literally lost their mind at her sight. As a result, this created some hate from a certain category of the feminine population. However, Nsona was beyond reproach. She drew men to her simply because she was a beautiful young woman. She was not responsible for that. She had never done anything wrong. She never gave in to any proposal despite the numerous pretenders, married or single. Be it to become a first, a second, a third spouse or more. Not even for some stolen moments with one or another of those who attempted to seduce her with many gifts.

The young woman happened to be proud; very proud. A pride that made her know what she did not want. But she had a little more difficulties to know what she wanted. That might had been the only reason that she could have been blamed for. But her education kept her within the limits to be respected with regard to her surroundings. Even if sometimes she played with the feelings of people, despite herself.

After having gone head up through the five hundred steps that separated her from her domicile, she arrived in the family yard, not forgetting to greet the many children that had welcomed her as the very star of the neighbourhood.

"Where have you been?" a raspy and nervous voice greeted her.

She did not answer immediately. Her uncle was not an easy man, but she had great respect for him as despite an ill-tempered nature he was good and just with her. However, he sometimes proved to be quite obstinate. He continued to talk to her.

"We have been waiting for you almost all morning. Have you forgotten we would be having visitors? Did not your mother tell you about them?"

Nsona did not dare to reply. She bowed her head, desperately looking for her uncle's spouse. The latter appeared at the entry of the home, with a calabash filled with water in the hands.

"Leave the child alone! I did not tell her anything. You know she would not have appreciated this pretender! Only your stubbornness to see him as a good alliance has set you in this shameful situation that made this poor man wait in vain. And overall, you made him hope for something impossible."

She buzzed after she had finished talking while her husband muttered inaudible words before backing into the house.

"Are they still here?" the young woman asked with a worried voice.

"Of course not. They have gone. They finally realized that they were wasting their time. Come over and help me."

"Sure, mama."

She walked towards the old woman and took the calabash from her hands.

The old couple had taken Nsona with them when she was only five years old. She had just lost her mother, Myezi, after a very sudden disease. Her father, Ogada, who had three wives had judged it better for her to go live with the elder brother of his deceased spouse who had never had any children himself. One day, the news spread around that Nsona's father had not come back from hunting. A buffalo hunting, which is one of the most dangerous ones. She had seen him very scarcely since she was born and only had a vague souvenir of him. She just remembered that he was known as someone not quite sympathetic.

Nsona called her uncle's wife « mama »; so was the custom. And really, this woman acted as a mother for her. She had always treated her like the daughter that she herself never had.

"Thank you, mama."

"What for, daughter?"

"You did tell me about the visitors. But I did not want to be here. Why should I have? To tell them that I had no interest for their son? Fortunately, uncle is not a fan of arranged marriages!"

"Oh yes, you may say so, because if he was, you would already be a housewife somewhere. Are you aware that only yesterday three delegations came around just for you?"

"Please, do not say more!" the young girl begged. I do not want to hear anymore about it."

Her mother rose up and laid her eyes on her.

"What a difficult young person you are! What are you hoping for? The perfect man? La perle rare? It has been months and I do not know how many men who come to see your uncle for your hand and you always make the same reply: « he is not the one for me »..."

She stopped talking, her eyes laid on the young girl.

"Just tell me how he will be, the one for you? How will you know he is the one? Can you tell me?"

The girl made no answer. She sighed and kept giving kitchen utensils to her daughter who kept her head bowed while she was storing the objects on the little table in front of her. She finally talked.

"I am not making a fuss, you know. Have not you ever had this feeling that needs you to see certain conditions to be fulfilled before accepting anything? For example ... "

She was not able to finish her sentenced. Quite worried, she quickly bent forward towards her mother who was holding her leg painfully.

" Mama, what is the matter? What is happening to you?"

The old woman did not answer and was prostrate for a little moment, strongly holding her daughter's hand. At last she rose up, slowly recovering her breath. She did not want her daughter to worry.

"Do not worry, it is over. I just twisted my knee when getting off my bed this morning."

"So you should go and rest, I shall do that. I can take care of this without you being there. Go and have a rest."

Her mother agreed.

"You are right. I shall lie down. But I shall stay outside. Please go and get me a mat, will you? That way I shall keep an eye on you."

The young girl had a light laugh.

"Oh, you exaggerate, mama! You taught me so many things I think I can make it without you keeping an eye on me."

She went into the house and came back out with a wonderful raffia mat that she laid delicately on the grass ground. Her mother slowly lay on it.

"All right, she said. So I shall just look at you."

She tenderly looked at the young woman who carried on with the work she had herself started that morning.

She had to add boiling water in the many containers in which there were some cloths being coloured. The tincture in some of them was too concentrated and it had to be diluted using a stick. It was a way to secure the full immersion of the knotted cloths.

Her mother, known in the hood as "ma" Kimani, had realized the feat to create an activity that had a reputation in the whole empire. A very good reputation. It was such that even the sovereign used to send some of his people to buy from her. Each time, he passed his command in advance and she created the best articles for him, as diverse and colourful as possible. She sold them at such a price that she could afford not to produce anything for several moons before deciding to gain some more money. Her latest production before the one in progress had been done some fifteen days before. It had been sold out the very day it had been available. Slowly, she was becoming famous even beyond the empire. But she refused to increase her production. She did not want to be trapped by the situation that could be engendered. She had seen some acquaintances become slaves of their own trade. They then did not feel any more pleasure when working.

Her little factory was not so big. She employed people, women or men, whenever the work needed it. The family yard was then in an uproar. There were many candidates despite the hardness of the job to be done. But ma Kimani was very generous and she cared for those she hired to work. She considered them as their skills deserved. She thus maintained their will to work and their level of performance in their duty.

The fact was that with an ambassador like Nsona, ma Kimani could only be known and more than that: recognized. Everyone new that the wonderful outfits that the young woman wore were made of cloths that her mother produced. So she never hesitated to be seen as much as she could to make them know especially when they showed new patterns.

"Anyway, you are right. That man was not the one for you. I shall tell you myself which one will suit you."

Having said that, the old woman turned on herself and decided to have some sleep.

*

Mbanza Miongo was a rather big village in the empire. Though it was landlocked between the ocean and a very powerful river, it was a traffic junction for numerous travellers who went back and forth through the empire and the regions around. Strangers came from everywhere. From the north or the south beyond the great river but also from the west, from the ocean. The small town was known to have abundant and very healthy cattle and fertile soil which produced tremendous quantities of vegetables, cereals and fruits. But one still had to go away from the city, beyond the hills that gave it its name in order to purchase game or any other wild animals. There were many foreign hunters who came to sell the fruits of their labour. Some of them led their activities rather smartly.

But the real speciality of the region was iron. This one was available everywhere in the empire and the clay that was used to create the different necessary tools to transform it was the best of all surrounding regions. Create and manufacture these tools was the job of "pa" Sadisa, Nsona's uncle. He had to go out of the city, southwards, when going to his workplace. Just like his wife, he worked only when he felt it necessary. He also sold his competencies very expensively.

Nsona grew up without any particular need. She had never lacked anything. Instead, she sometimes, even nowadays, had too much for her alone. Food, clothes, tenderness, family love. She had been filled during all the time she grew up. Was it to help her bear the death of her mother that the couple treated her so well? Or was it to help her forget that she was no longer with her father, who also came to decease some time later? However, this abundance full way of life made her become very demanding on whatever her personal wellness. Maybe she now feared to lack this comfort in a marriage that would not match with the standards of life she had always had. This would explain her difficulties to accept a pretender despite all those who had presented themselves. Even if among them some would have been a good bargain.

Pa Sadisa and his spouse had only treated the young child so for her good. Now she was a young woman and they saw in her behaviour her will to make the right choice. Even the old man, despite his very bad temper, was rather patient on that with her. He welcomed all demands with great enthusiasm and if at certain times he seemed to force her hand, he knew that he would never push to a choice that would not be her own.

So he played his role with seriousness and devotion. His wife, let alone his daughter, did not know that he took time to investigate on all the pretenders that came around, as well as on their families. Each time he received a demand, he took care to set a meeting date that was away enough so he could know more on the origins and the members of the clans involved.

In his trade, he had to meet a lot of people, and he had made a speciality to establish ties with most of his professional interlocutors. He even used his skills to thank those who provided him with useful information. He could get to do a little more complete work without asking for extra payment. An exchange of services in a way.

Therefore, he would cancel a reception if the information he had received did not go in the required way. He would find a compelling pretext to make the claimant and his family understand that it would be pointless to go further in their approach. Quite some times, he would evoke the young woman's scepticism about the proposed union. He did so with such skill that there had never been any resentment from the unsuccessful suitors or their families. That was a great proof of his sense of diplomacy. Indeed, a refusal of marital union was not always a smooth move. Honour...

Pa Sadisa was thus known far beyond Mbanza Miongo for his work, but also because he was known as the father of one of the most beautiful women of the empire. Therefore, he concluded some of his deals thanks to the hope that some might have had to get closer to his daughter through him. But while concluding his affairs, he made it clear to his interlocutors that under no circumstances could he influence a decision from the young woman. Some understood the man, others less, believing that as a father he had all rights to decide who his daughter was to marry. To which he replied that he could at least only counsel, then recommending to the claimant to rely on the will of the almighty and the ancestors. But this situation was still beginning to weigh him, and he hoped deep inside that the young woman would find a party as soon as possible so that his wife and he would get some quietness.

*

For the rest of the morning, Nsona continued to do the work her mother had let her do. This was not the first time it happened. Most of the time, when there was a lot of work, ma Kimani hired employees. Nsona only gave a hand when she felt like it. She came, worked a little, left for one reason or another, and then came back again. And so on. But when there was only her mother and herself, she did not skimp and gladly took all the work into her own account, asking the latter to rest or to take care of something else.

Some people who did not know this facet of her personality took her for a lazy facetious young woman. Others, who hated her for attracting the attention of all the men, deliberately ignored her laudable side and emphasized the one that could be more reprehensible.

There was only one other young woman of her age who accepted Nsona as she was and who was really sincere with her. It was her best friend, Lukuayi. She clearly portrayed her name because she always had something to say. She was born in the house next door and had grown up with her. Normally, she would be at her side helping her have the job done. But Lukuayi had married a few moons earlier and was now less available for her friend. She had left the neighbourhood to join her husband in a nearby village, a few hours of walk away from Mbanza Miongo, beyond the hills. After the marriage of her friend, the father of the latter had not hesitated to tell Nsona's that if she did not marry very quickly, it would become a source of serious problems. It was not the first time he had told him that. Since the marriage and departure of Lukuayi, the two young women had seen each other only two or three times.

It was an important change in Nsona's life. Having grown up with her friend, having being used to see her every day and suddenly brought to see her only once in a while. It was difficult and this situation had slowly become unbearable to her. Although she did not realize it, a feeling of loneliness had begun to overwhelm her. Her best friend had chosen a young man from a good family, although from a lower social class than hers. She had said that she had found happiness when she expected it the least. Indeed, she thought that she still had a few years of celibacy to live. But Lukuayi had said that before a delegation came to make a demand for Nsona. Among the many visitors that came with Nsona's pretender, there was the future husband of her best friend. He had noticed the young woman and had come back a few moons later with determination. He had come back to visit the young woman a few times and had seduced her. So he had come later with his family to conclude a rather sudden but very strong union. Lukuayi's clan had discovered that in the past her husband's had been of a great help to hers. With time, the events of the past had slowly been erased from people's mind. But in the case of a wedding an investigation was always made to know who was the pretender, who was the future bride and it was a tradition to visit the "guardians of the community's memory". These characters of the empire were the ones that were questioned when information was required on a family.

They were some kind of living encyclopaedias, able to provide ancient information that was forgotten by most of the people. As often, this trade was transmitted from father to son, or from mother to daughter. This meant that each guardian started his learning very early, well before he was a teenager and collected a tremendous amount of knowledge. This was about the relationships and the links between the different families and the clans they derived from. It was a noble trade that was greatly respected and gave great credibility to the words coming from it. A guardian only gave out information and facts, and never in any case did he give an advice on any family or any clan. They had a duty of reserve. Once the information was transmitted, it was up to the applicant to decide what to do.

For Lukuayi and her bridegroom, nothing had come against their wedding. In certain other cases some old conflict came to prevent any further action towards a union. Sometimes, for the good of the suitors there were meetings that were organised between the families to solve a never ending dispute or ignore it, deciding that it belonged to the past. But in other situations some stubborn uncle could be enough to stop a marriage that would have made young people happy.

That day, Nsona was once more working on her mother's cloths while thinking of her best friend. She had a feeling of satisfaction knowing her happy with her choice and her new life.

As for her, she hoped to meet happiness. She now hoped to meet it in a not too long schedule.

2

Mbanza Miongo was a quite big village in a great empire. It was quite a trading little city in which hundreds of merchants of all kinds came to sell this and that. It could be simple objects or precious jewellery but also head of cattle, or clothing, salt or wild game. But the type of traders changed according to the seasons. The same were not visible at the same time. They came by waves. The selling zones were defined on the whole territory according to the different specialties.

In the neighbourhood of Nsona's family, according to the season it was possible to find rare fish or wild game traders. They were the most of the sellers in the market through which Nsona usually walked when she went wandering in the streets around her house. The great show occurred when some traders came in some rare times with wild game captured alive. They were sold for special events in which the buyers wanted to have fresh meat. So the beasts had to be killed as late as possible. The procession that occurred in those times attracted all the inhabitants around to see pass by animals that in any other case they would have seen only dead, skinned and most often dried or smoked.

On these occasions, meetings were held, reunions happened. Merchants sometimes returned from one rainy season to the next or did not reappear before several seasons. No one ever worried about that because it was a very common practice. Other merchants had been coming for generations, some having resumed the succession of family activity. There were also newcomers, merchants that had never seen before, who came back regularly in town. Others came once, and then disappeared forever. It was said that they were certainly spirits who wanted to offer themselves a final crowd bath before leaving definitely for the city of ancestors.

This was even more confirmed when, after an investigation, the guardians of the collective memory were unable to provide any information about one of them. It was therefore rather logical that the concerned would never reappear. But how could one be sure that the error was not on the side of the guardians of the collective memory? No one could say it with any certainty. Everyone could therefore prefer the version that suited him best.

That day, old Sadisa walked back home from a hard day's intense work and was eager to find himself in his house to taste the delicious meal that his beloved wife would have prepared for him. He did not know what that would be, but he knew that whatever it was, he would feast. Mother Kimani was an excellent cook. She had also passed on this gift to their daughter. The mother and the girl sometimes had fun to make him guess who had prepared the meal. When he found the answer, it was often due to luck because he was not able to distinguish the cooking hand from either one. The other times he avoided the challenge, simply meaning that as long as what was on his plate was delicious, he did not bother which of both had done the cooking.

"Sadisa!"

He raised his head, surprised he was by the tone of the voice. It seemed hostile to him. The face he discovered before him confirmed his first impression. It was that of a man who did not seem to be in front of him to talk in a friendly way or even to sympathize. Yet he did not seem to know him. Why would a stranger want to attack him so? But the fact that he called him in such a way, directly by his name without taking care to add a qualifier of respect, did not bode well. Only a friend could have spoken to him so. Obviously, he was not.

"That is me all right," he answered. "How can I help you, my friend? "

The man looked at him for a short moment before speaking up.

"You disrespected my family! You will have to arrange that in a way or another."

He had spoken very loudly. This attracted the attention of passers-by around them. A feeling of curiosity now floated in the air.

"I do not understand," old Sadisa stammered.

"You don't understand? I am going to refresh your memory."

Some onlookers had gathered around them, feeling that something unusual was happening. The man then began to express the substance of his thought.

"You kept my people waiting for almost a whole morning when you had to introduce them to your daughter. That is not acceptable. If I had been there myself..."

Old Sadisa interrupted him.

"Forgive me, but... I still do not understand. All those who came to and left my home have done so on good terms with me, without any reproach or animosity. So who are you exactly?"

"Yes, who are you?" a voice asked among the onlookers who were now closer.

In Mbanza Miongo, many people knew each other. Old Sadisa was all the more known because he had a function that made him meet a lot of people. Among those who had come close, there were a few people who had found it strange that someone would behave so with him and who were willing not to let it be. The man felt it and seemed to lower the tone slightly. But his intentions did not change all the same.

"Of course, no one ever has any reason to blame you. But they are all weak and two days ago my brother was particularly weak in leaving without even seeing the young woman whom her son coveted. What a feat! And we should let that go?"

"But I had informed your brother that it was no use coming along, but he did not want to hear anything."

"If I had been there myself, things would have happened otherwise. You will soon hear from our family, because I am not the only one who has not appreciated this humiliation that my brother had accepted to endure."

Father Sadisa did not even have to reply. The onlookers who had gathered decided to answer the belligerent.

"Are you not ashamed to seek conflict?" a first man asked him.

"It is always the same thing," another one said. "Those who are really concerned have not made any problems and it is you who comes to stir the fire!!"

"Particularly if you look at it well, you are certainly on the sidelines of this family of which you claim to defend the honour!!"

"Yes, because if you were really in tune with your brother, you would not allow yourself such a behaviour!"

"This means that you do not even respect him, nor his son!"

"That is true! So what do you want, finally? Compensation? You are a profiteer, quick to amplify a so-called problem to benefit from it!! Disappear!! You bird of ill omen!"

Father Sadisa had nothing more to say. The crowd had been responsible for reducing the unfriendly character that had attacked him. It had been a very bad idea from the man to do it in the middle of the street in front of everyone, while the old man was still a character in the vicinity.

"Go! And do not show up around here again!" a man shouted out while the individual was walking away.

Many of the onlookers then gathered around old Sadisa to comfort and support him. One of them made himself a spokesperson.

"Do not worry, elder one. He is just a profiteer. He is not going to do anything more than to bother you in the street like he just did. He has understood that if he goes after you, he would go after a lot more people than he thinks. He will think twice before going to search problems to you and your family."

"Thank you to all!" father Sadisa replied. "I shall also contact this brother he is referring to in order to know exactly who he is. I cannot think that this man can knowingly let this so-called brother behave like this. Thank you again for your presence at my side."

"Do not worry, we shall always be there!"

"Thank you all!" Nsona's father said one last time before returning to his way home.

But this little episode nevertheless had shaken him. He was thinking that this kind of thing could have happened more often. He even said to himself it should have happened sooner. Indeed, the number of refusals he had had to oppose to an equally imposing number of suitors could have been the consequence. Among these, some filled with hopes awkwardly maintained by a sometimes unsettled attitude, not to say immature of Nsona, who did not always know how to put a clear and definite term to certain advances.

He thought of what his neighbour had told him sometimes about his daughter and hoped that his words would remain a dead letter. But at his age, he knew that anything could happen, even the worst. And most often, the worst happened when you did not expect it.

*

When he arrived at home, he did what he usually did. He started by taking a good bath. Then he put on his favourite tunic, which smelled so good and fresh. His wife always prepared him clothes for his return at night. She was exceptional in taking care of him. He always found an excellent dish to recover the strength he had lost during his day of hard work. But she worked hard too. So he strove to return the favour as best he could. He did so first by finding reliable people to work on the cloths. By word of mouth, his networks allowed him to know where to find good men. But beyond that, he made himself the most congenial he could with her, despite a rather grumpy temper. And it was not easy for him. On the contrary, it was a real feat that he achieved for her.

Sitting on a long carved wooden chair in the courtyard, he sipped a large cup of sugar cane wine with delight. From where he was placed, he had a view on the street and could see almost all the passersby rushing one way and the other. He watched all the faces and strove with amusement to figure out what they expressed. There was fatigue, most often, impatience also or then slight irritation. After a day of hard work, it was no wonder to see this on faces. Yet, he detected all this in an atmosphere imbued with serene tranquillity, or even a restrained joy. There were calls that were occasionally launched on the fly between individuals who were crossing or finding each other. Sometimes they could be individuals who did not know each other in any way, but who found in a few moments a reason to sympathize, only for the time of an exchange of a few words.

The inhabitants of Mbanza Miongo had all possible reasons to be at peace with one another. They lived in a prosperous country, they had everything they needed, and when it was necessary, the authorities did everything useful to preserve the stability of the empire. Mbanza Miongo belonged in fact to one of the half a dozen provinces that constituted it. Each of these provinces referred to the imperial authority, and each provincial authority had under its responsibility several chiefs-places that were subject to them. There were occasionally some adventurers who spread fear on the roads of the Empire, but they were quickly brought back to a much better behaviour.

"Good evening, have you had a good day?"

His wife, Kimani, had just entered the courtyard and had approached him with a rather serious look. He looked at her for a brief moment before answering her back.

"Yes, thank you. What about you?"

"Yes, me too. I did not have much to do. It is pretty quiet for me nowadays. I have just got back from the family at the corner of the street. They are in the middle of misfortune. Their eldest son, Sambu, fell from a palm tree this morning. He is in a very worrying state. In addition to his fall, a pack of palm nuts fell on him, and seriously wounded him at the hip because of the quills. The poor boy is suffering martyrdom.

Father Sadisa sighed.

"What a misfortune! Such a promising boy!"

"Whom our daughter had also turned away."

"Oh, please stop, I do not really see what link there is."

"There is no link, indeed. It is just a statement. Who knows if this has not distracted him since?

Bringing him to make a mistake at the top of this tree and fall so.”

“That is it! Keep saying this type of hypothesis and the wind helping, you will see that soon everyone will say the same thing. Then you will be the first to complain that people blame your daughter!”

“ I am not formulating a hypothesis, my dear. The wind has already done its work and I am just repeating what some people are already saying. I heard it involuntarily.”

Having said this, she slipped away into the abode.

On his side, father Sadisa finished sipping his cane wine, rose and went to visit the neighbours around the corner to give them his moral support.

On his way, as he approached the wounded boy's home, he crossed his daughter. He read on her face the expression of diffuse pain. The situation was therefore more serious than what Kimani had described to him. His eyes crossed those of the young woman and he understood without her telling him anything. The irreversible had occurred. He took her by the shoulders as she could barely hold back her tears.

“You have nothing to reproach yourself, my child. You are not responsible for anything. Life is so made and everyone has to accept it as it is. Everyone has to make decisions and assume them and their consequences. He had decided to declare himself to marry you; you opposed a refusal, which was your right. You have nothing to be blamed for. Now go home and do not get out. That is the best to do for now. Do you hear me?"

"Yes, papa. I am going home."

He watched her go her way for another few dozen steps. He entered the concession whose head of family was of his acquaintances since childhood. He threw a circular glance. There were not many people. Most of the visitors had left so as to return in the evening in order to attend the wake that would take place as soon as the night would come.

He walked towards the front door of the family home, from which there was an impressive silence for the event. In normal times, incessant cries and crying would have been heard either outside or inside the walls. But this time, nothing resonated. As he was about to lift the linen curtain that obstructed the entrance, a woman came out. She stopped abruptly at his sight.

"Good evening, mother Aïssa," he said.

She stared at him briefly. Then she turned away and lowered her head. As if she wanted to run away from his eyes.

"Good evening," old Sadisa.

She walked away as quickly as she had appeared. What a strange behaviour, he thought. He would not wait long to know the reason of it.

He went through the opening and arrived directly in a great room where the greatest part of the concerned family was. The young man's body was in the very middle. A white shroud covered it, stained with the blood that had dipped from the wound. Father Sadisa had his eyes still despite of himself on this inert body, which was still that morning that of a young fellow filled with dynamism and future.

What had happened? Why was life so cruel as to blow up such a beautiful promise of life?

He moved a few steps closer before seeing a shadow rise right in front of him.

"Get out of here! It is your child who… !"

"You be quiet ! You cheeky boy ! Have a little respect for your poor brother's memory!"

The man who had intervened pulled strongly the young man by the arm and brought him aside, thus being himself in the way. He slowly moved aside to let father Sadisa move on. The latter advanced to the wicker bed that bore the deceased. He crouched down and had a short low prayer. He stood up slowly, his eyes fixed on the young man's still face, which seemed to be that of a man sleeping peacefully.

He then had a strange sensation. He raised his head and looked around. In the darkness of the room, all eyes were on him. What he saw in them was no sympathy or recognition for his presence on the scene at this painful moment. Instead, these glances showed distrust and misunderstanding. There was also and above all anger. He remembered his wife's words, and then Nsona's tears. He decided not to stay. He knew that he was undesired and that only the recent occurrence of the event prevented the situation from becoming somewhat uncomfortable for him.

He walked towards the exit and then crossed the courtyard as silently as he had arrived. Now he knew he had to be wary of these neighbours. But above all, he now had a duty that was more than ever that of a father. He had to protect his daughter because she was obviously held by this family responsible for the death of their son. As he knew how people were led to interpret certain situations or meddle in what was none of their business, he knew that Nsona should keep a low profile for a while. Same for his wife and for himself. He then thought of the man who had stopped him earlier in the street. Was he informed of this accident? Was there any connection between these two situations? What if, arguing of this sad epilogue in the life of this boy, other families who had been refused by his daughter came to make him bear all their misfortunes? What was going on? The quietness of their little life was going to be put to the test and he knew it. He would have to deal with it. But he was ready. All his life, he had faced all kinds of situations. This time again he would face it, protecting his wife and daughter.

*

That following night, Nsona was unable to sleep. She remembered again and again the body of the young man and the blood that colored the shroud that covered him. This face that she had seen so often since her childhood and which had given her such beautiful smiles, she would have preferred never to see it so still. She would have preferred to keep the smiling memory of the advances he had made to her so many times. He never wanted to believe that she would push him away as they had dated as children. But this was common for children living in the same area, whose parents knew each other and spoke to each other regularly for one reason or another. Parents who also went as far as visiting each other.

When they had became teenagers, they had kept dating and over time Nsona had had more and more effect on the young man. She had always been friendly with him. Perhaps that was what had encouraged him to reveal himself. But the young woman had never seen her childhood friend as anything other than a simple comrade who lived in the same environment as her. Yet she did not feel offended when he declared his keen attraction to her. She had considered it as a game. She was wrong. On his side, Sambu was very serious and thought hard that by formalizing the situation, involving the parents, she would be influenced and would yield under social pressure. But that was not the case. He had underestimated the girl's strong character. When he had realized his failure, it was too late. Everyone around them knew it, from all their childhood comrades to all their parents. Everyone had understood that it had been a great blow of fate and had compassion for him. This attitude was unbearable to him. He would have preferred to be mocked rather than complained about.

He had begun by closing himself off, speaking to very few people outside his loved ones. He walked head down, avoiding other people's eyes. At first, it had been thought to be transient. It was believed that he would recover and become the jovial and welcoming young man that everyone knew. Indeed, little by little he had become himself again, to the satisfaction of all. What courage he had had to overcome such a slap.

But what people ignored was that the pain was deeper than it seemed. And no one had been able to probe it. The young man had been able to bluff in order to put an end to the ambient compassion that was unbearable to him. But deep inside, he had even less bore to be repelled by the young woman. He had never recovered from it. From that moment on, he had begun to have periods of distraction in everything he did. He had previously avoided the disastrous consequences this could have had on some of his activities. His relatives had realized this, but they hoped that with time and the help of the spirits, it would fade. But in spite of themselves, they more or less turned a blind eye on the situation, by fear of hurting if they told him about his condition. That was a fatal mistake for the young man. Today, they had to find a person who would be responsible for this situation. That would give them good conscience. And that responsible person would be a she.

Nsona knew that now. She had gone at the young man's bedside as soon as she had heard the news of the accident. She had been upset and had put aside any apprehension to go to his house. After all, she suspected that some in his family had not appreciated her refusal to marry him. She therefore did not ignore that she would maybe not be welcome. When she had arrived, the young man was still alive. When she had seen him, she had understood that he was in a very serious condition. The silence in the room was an impressive testimony to this.

He had smiled when he had seen her, as if he had only waited for her to arrive. She had taken his hand and crouched next to him. After exchanging a long look, he had spoken.

"I do not blame you, you know...."

She then had silent sobs.

"I am sorry, Sambu... So sorry..."

"I do not blame you..." he whispered again.

They had remained so, hand in hand, for a while that had seemed an eternity to the young woman. She had bowed her head and closed her eyes. Then she had felt the embrace of the young man's hand loosen. She had then opened her eyes only to find that those of the injured young man had closed. Definitely. Only the boy's father had stood up to find out that his son no longer was. The outcome was so obviously awaited that no reaction happened from anyone in the room.

Silently, shaken by such a distress and an unspeakable guilt, Nsona had risen to leave the room. Instinctively, she knew it was better for her not to stay around. She had left, dazed, walking the streets until she had met her father.

*

She had been in bed for a long time. Through the canvas of the heavy cloth hanging from her door, she saw the glow of a torch approaching. She recognized her mother's walk. She straightened up on her diaper as a head pushed the fabric back and appeared.

"Are you sleeping, my child?"

"No, mama, I am not asleep. I just cannot. What happened is terrible. I keep thinking that Sambu died because of me. Do you realize he knew he was going to die and he still wanted to tell me he did not blame me?"

Mother Kimani sat down next to Nsona and passed her arm around her shoulders. In the darkness, the dancing glow of the torch drew intriguing arabesques on their faces.

"You must not feel guilty. It is your right to choose the one you want as your husband. It is not an obligation to say yes to the first comer."

"But he was not a first comer! We almost grew up together!" the young woman insisted.

"Well, in that case you should have accepted his demand."

This answer that the young woman did not expect surprised her. That was her mother's goal.

"Hum?! If you believe what you are saying now and you think that it would have been a good enough reason, why did you push him away then?"

There was a moment of silence. Nsona understood. She had to put herself together. If she ever had this attitude outside home, someone would soon be quick to condemn her even more. Whatever her own opinion of the situation, she would have to appear detached and dignified. After all, she was not the first young woman who had refused one or more marriages.

Her mother looked at her straight in the eye.

"So be strong and face this moment, my daughter. In life, there are difficult moments to overcome and this is one of them. Be sure that you will certainly have some more in your life; and perhaps even more difficult. We are here for you, with you, you are not alone. Never forget that. Now go to sleep."

The old woman got up with some difficulty. She complained of chest pain before leaving the room to go to bed, letting the young woman do the same.

3

Father Sadisa's family did not attend the young man's funeral. It took place the next day, within the family concession. Indeed, according to custom and belief, the dead never left completely. Thus, by keeping their remains close to their living place, they were allowed not to be disoriented. But the truth was that the living found it difficult seeing their loved ones leave and thus used this pretext to bury them as close as possible to themselves. Cemeteries did not exist.

The crowd that had gathered to attend the ceremony was so big that it had overflowed to the small wooden flap that symbolically blocked the access to the courtyard.

At first, by mid-morning, Nsona had sat in front of the house, near the entrance. She was clearly visible to all who passed by. Little by little, she realized that the eyes were increasingly insistent on her and often hostile. She had also noticed that some people were walking back looking in her direction. By staying there, she had become an attraction. To keep a low profile also meant to keep out reach of the eyes of the curious ones.

The family of the young deceased man had made the rumor that she was responsible for his death. This idea had spread beyond the family yard and was beginning to go around the agglomeration. But different opinions were heard. Some abounded in the way of the family, others were more lucid and tried to make it clear that if every time a young woman refused to marry the suitor had to die, then many young men would no longer be in this world. So people should leave this girl alone. But her detractors were still the most numerous. People always like to find culprits for all sorts of reasons.

So, what Father Sadisa had feared happened. A few families, whose son, a suitor of marriage to Nsona had been turned away, began to make it known a few days later that he was no longer himself. He would have become as possessed. His spirit was said to be held captive by the young woman. Another one would have lost all taste for life and would spend his time around graves to converse with the deceased in order to see them prepare for his arrival. In short, he was said to have lost his mind. The least damning accusations were the lack of involvement and the decline in performance of the so designated young men in their daily activities. This would have been noticed since the refusal from Father Sadisa's family.

This young woman with an incredible beauty, everyone knew that, had an excessive pride. It was this fault that made her systematically refuse any marriage.

"She thinks no man is good enough for her!"

"Yes, and it seems that a genie roams around her!"

"Certainly not! You do not get it! She is a witch! She cannot be married!!"

"Absolutely! That is why her mother who gave birth to her got rid of her with her father's coward complicity."

"What do you mean? Are they not her real parents?! So everything is understandable, now: this girl is disturbed!!"

Speculations went on strongly, each more distant than the other from the truth. Slanders were tenacious and devastating. They had made a very undeserved reputation to the young woman. It had even began to spread out beyond Mbanza Miongo. Those who pushed the rumor to the extreme were women. There were, of course, those who were jealous of her beauty because they were not as successful as she was with men. But there were also sisters who wanted revenge for having seen their brother humiliated, according to them. Nsona had become unhappy. Her feelings, of course, reflected on mother Kimani and father Sadisa.

The couple could see that their beloved daughter was very affected by the situation. And that worried them. What effects could these rumors have on the young woman with time? Of course, she had a rather strong character, but what was happening was exceptional and every human being has his limits. Even the strongest one. They feared she would be severely disturbed.

Every day, they did everything they could to distract or keep her busy. That day, they had welcomed her best friend, Lukuayi. A few moons later, she decided to come and spend a few days with Nsona.

"How are you, sweetheart? Ma Kimani told me that you have certainly had better days."

"You know, ma Kimani sometimes exaggerates things. I am not doing very well, that is true, but I think I am still going to make it."

Lukuayi had known her friend since they were small. She also knew when she was in good shape or not. At this moment, she knew that she was trying to bluff her.

"Do you really think I am going to believe you so easily? You seem to forget who I am. Well, I am going to have to make you change ideas. Come on, let us go for a walk. You do not have to stay locked up like this every day because of a happening you are not responsible for."

In spite of herself, Nsona got up and followed her friend. They walked for a long time talking about one thing and another, but particularly about Lukuayi's new life as a wife. She had a pleasant life, with a loving husband who filled her with an unfailing presence. He would leave from time to time for a few days because of his activity. He marketed salt that was harvested on an island not far from Mbanza Miongo. He had managed to create a distribution network and this allowed him to support his family well. He had even asked his father not to tire himself any more because he was earning enough for him to rest in his last years.

They arrived at the riverbank. The first houses were a few hundred steps away because of the occasional floods that could occur. There were children playing at the water's edge, others bathed a few cables from the shore. They were not to go too far from the shore because the mouth to the ocean was not very far away, and very sudden and strong currents could occur. Dramas had already happened. They were attributed to the genies of the river. Upstream, a few men were cleaning some fishing utensils and a little further upstream, women were busy around stalls drying fish.

They stopped a few steps from the water. Nsona's gaze was lost on the calm waters, which however had a very noticeable power. She turned her eyes towards her friend.

"Lukuayi, do you know what the most difficult thing is for me?"

"I am listening to you."

Nsona took a deep breath.

"Since Sambu passed away, since some people make me be considered as a witch and put all the evils of the world on my back...."

The young bachelor stopped talking and again let her gaze wander beyond the waters. Suddenly feeling her on the verge of tears, Lukuayi leaned towards her. She took her by the shoulders.

"What are you trying to tell me, Nsona? Please talk to me."

" ...there is not a single marriage proposal for me any more. Do you realize that? It has been several moons already and no one comes for me anymore. My father does not see anyone anymore, I do not even have the opportunity to choose anyone!"

"Come on, please stop. It is just a bad time to pass. I know it is because of the rumors that were made about you, but this period will stop, believe me!"

"I have had enough! I am tired of this situation! I am going to marry the first one who shows up! I can assure you of that."

Lukuayi widened her eyes.

"Will you stop rambling?! What is wrong with you saying something like that? Do you realize that?"

"Well, I am saying so because that is what I am going to do and I will do it!"

"Hey! You really are not well!" her friend outraged. "What if the evil spirits ever heard you and had someone come to you? Take that off right now, can you hear me? Withdraw those words now!

Nsona fell silent, looking again above the waters.

"Withdraw them now, I am telling you!" Lukuayi insisted. "Imagine if your words were picked up by an evil spirit?"

The disillusioned young woman turned her eyes.

"You are right," she said with a smile. "I withdraw what I just said. I will take as long as it takes."

She took her friend in her arms.

"It is a good thing you are here, fortunately. Otherwise I could do anything that goes through my mind."

They decided to go home. On the way back, Lukuayi was uncomfortable. She saw her friend in a difficult psychic state and compared it to the happiness she lived on her side. Moreover, she had not told her friend how happy she herself was. She had only recently known she was pregnant and had not dared to tell Nsona. She had wondered how she would have taken it. If she had known that it would have done her the greatest good, she would not have hesitated. Instead, she abstained. Talking to her friend would have done the latter the best.

*

A few days after her best friend had left, the situation had worsened in old Sadisa's house. Half a dozen families claiming to have been harmed by the girl had come to bring old Sadisa to account. He was faced with a duty to go to the justice officer to defend his family, to defend his daughter. He would attend public hearings on the large square in which he would justify himself over and over again, often under the jibes of an audience that would necessarily be hostile in its great majority. A lot of time and energy, as such, to be spent. But it did not matter. His daughter had the right to say no to whoever she wanted and everything had always been done with respect for each of the families who had come forward. He would face, as always in all the restrictive situations he had had. With the support of his wife he had always faced.

But in these parts of the world, there is always the extended family, the clan, which supports its own. In fact, Sadisa had seen his brothers, including the children of his uncles, and others join him in defending him. Some long-time friends had also decided to support them. Friends who had over time almost become members of the family.

That day, all were gathered in the backyard of the family parcel at father Sadisa's. It was a question of making a status of the current situation, analyze the already known complaints, and putting in place a strategy to defend before the justice officer. But it was also necessary to anticipate which other families might be tempted to take advantage of the situation. Father Sadisa had a very clear memory of those who had come to his house to marry his daughter. He therefore had no difficulty in quoting potential opportunists. He thought that the real people concerned, namely the close relatives of the young people who had been turned away, would not have the indelicacy of attacking him and his family. Instead, he feared those who gravitated around them. It was often the father's distant brothers, who saw this as an opportunity to value themselves easily under the pretext of defending the honor of the son and the family, often pushed by wives who were in search of recognition.

"We need to know if some of them have already behaved in this way," the eldest of the family said. "We must be wary of those who make of this kind of situation a trade fund. There are people who are indelicate enough to behave so."

"This is well known and justice officers often unmask this kind of maneuver," Sadisa said." I think we should not care about that."

"Particularly since for most of these "aggrieved" it has been several rainy seasons since the case was closed and everyone, just as us, has moved on."

The last one who had spoken had knowingly insisted that anyone had been harmed. He was the youngest member of the meeting, but yet had a long life experience. He often gave relevant opinions that his elders followed very smartly. He was the one who had suggested that all should move in with father Sadisa for the duration of this situation. This was also in order to show Nsona that the clan was in solidarity and that he did not abandon her. He kept talking.

"But we must still be careful and not over-trust because the justice officer is only a man and who knows what can influence him in one way or another."

Another one nodded.

"Indeed, Indeed, Ebata, we must be careful, very careful. Those who attack us will also have their arguments."

At that very moment, a voice was heard from the entrance of the courtyard on the other side of the house. Ma Kimani stood up and went to see what was happening. She returned a few moments later with her hands slapping her cheeks in a stunned gesture. She beckoned her husband to join her. They chatted for a few moments before disappearing together towards the entrance of the courtyard. They all watched them go, intrigued. They reappeared moments later, pa Sadisa ahead. He immediately spoke to the small assembly.

"Family, I have to tell you about some unexpected good news. Good news but still intriguing."

He was silent for a moment. All eyes were on him and one could read the impatience on each of the faces.

"There is a delegation out there which is coming forward for a topic of the utmost importance."

The night was beginning to fall. Everyone looked at each other, a little disconcerted. A very discreet murmur was heard. Some noted that they were not ready to receive a delegation that had not been announced beforehand. Indeed, it was necessary to get prepared to receive such guests with all honors because one never knew what follow-up could come up. Others spoke of what was of course the most surprising: the late moment at which these emissaries showed up.

"Do we know them?" Pa Ebata asked.

"No, cadet, we do not know them", pa Sadisa replied, turning towards his wife with an interrogative look. "For sure, I did not recognize anyone."

"Neither did I," Ma Kimani said. "I did not recognize any of them."

There was a silence. It would be difficult to send visitors back without receiving them when they did not know them, despite the late hour. Everyone understood that. They had to prepare to welcome them. The elder of the clan, named Yinda, took matters into hand.

"What do they want? Hurry up, put those seats around here. By the way, how many are they?"

"A good half-dozen," a woman who had just gone for a curiosity walk on the other side replied.

"So it should be fine, there are not too many of them. We are much more than they are, so we can share what we have to eat. Those of us who are very hungry will not be satisfied tonight!"

This joke made many laugh. Very quickly, the courtyard was redesigned to place the visitors in front of their guests. A few moments later, the place became a meeting place between the two parties. Hands shook together, knees bent in sign of respect. There were two women and five men who made up the group of visitors. They took their seats and waited patiently, knowing that they were embarrassing their guests by arriving unexpectedly.

At last, everyone was settled and ready to talk. The eldest of the clan rose and silence came naturally.

"First of all, we welcome you. It is always a joy to welcome visitors. Thank you for your visit. We also ask you to forgive us in the somewhat improvised way we receive you."

He kept silent for a few moments, his hands clasped; his gaze was on the comers.

"Our ancestors said "It is up to the owner of the pirogue to show where to tie it." So we shall let you have the floor. We thank you."

He sat down, making way for the visitors' spokesman.

"We thank you all. Our ancestors also said, "When you go visit someone, do not let your pride cross the river with you." Everything you offer us will make us happy because we know that we have arrived unexpectedly and we ask you to please forgive us. Forgive us also for arriving so late because the reason is that we are passing through Mbanza Miongo and must leave tomorrow morning for Songo, where we come from. Business brought us here and a few moments ago, we did not even know we would be at your doorstep. Once more, please do forgive us."

At these words, deaf clapping of hands sounded as acquiescence. The woman who had spoken was the eldest of the visitors. She wore a midnight blue ensemble made of a wide skirt covering her feet and an equally wide top that went down to mid thighs. A kind of scarf of the same fabric was thrown carelessly over her shoulder. Another piece of the fabric was tied on her head. Graying braids overflowed, falling down. The fabric was of a quality that was not affordable to all. As a connoisseur, ma Kimani identified it so. The woman had gold bracelets on her wrists, completed with a necklace made with the same material. Clinging to the fabric on his head, a pendant covered the middle of her forehead. In the increasing darkness, it was difficult to figure out what it represented. All of this woman showed a high-ranking social origin. The people who accompanied her were no worse off in terms of clothing. One could distinguish silk or raffia with a very elaborate appearance in the clothing they wore. Gold jewelry also adorned the arms and heads.

"So, where should we tie the pirogue?" the woman said with a smile. "Well, I would like you to know that we have a son. He told us very late today that there is a reason here in your home to meet you, a reason that can only bring joy to our two families. He told us about a young girl. "Dear parents, I am interested in a young woman whose name is Nsona and lives with her father, who himself is named Father Sadisa." That is what our boy told us. As we already know that we are indeed at Father Sadisa's house, we only have to be confirmed that the young woman Nsona is indeed his daughter and, above all, that she is truly to be married. Thank you."

She sat down. Old Yinda stood up, clasped his hands and carried them to his mouth. He seemed to be thinking. He knew the situation was pretty new. To present oneself in this way for a wedding situation at the end of the day was unusual. Usually, this happened long before sunset. Besides, what did the visitors really want? They came from a far away land, they knew very well that it was not possible to give them an answer so early as tonight. Would they leave an emissary on the spot to notify them of their decision? In this case, how long would they be willing to wait for a decision?

"My sister, we have heard what you have just told us. We can confirm that we do have a young girl who answers to the name Nsona and is to be married. But before we go any further, if you will, we need to talk to ourselves because, as you must know, the situation is very special."

All visitors rose as a sign of respect to let their guests go in a conciliabule.

"We do understand that," the spokeswoman said. It is even normal to consult, so please do."

"Thank you so much."

He then went to the entrance of the house while most of the clan followed him. He passed the entrance and waited for everyone to join him, leaving a few people to stay with the guests.

"What a situation, really!" one of the women in the group whispered. "What a situation!"

"Yes, do you realize? Songo!! We are not going to let our daughter go there!! No, never! It is really too far! It takes at least half a moon's walk to get there!"

Tension was palpable.

"In addition, they arrived not only unexpectedly but, above all, late! Where do they really come from? Their explanations do not suit me. And we do not know much about this land from which they come."

For a few minutes, other expressions of opposition to this unexpected presence and its reason followed. Old Yinda waited calmly and silently for everyone to be somewhat free of their emotions.

"So, I see that we all have a reaction of rejection due to the circumstances. This is an unannounced and late arrival. I ask all of us to calm down because we will have to look beyond that. We are going to have to see what is our child's best interests in this case.

He turned to Father Sadisa.

"Cadet, have you heard of such a situation in any way? Did Nsona tell you or Ma Kimani about such a possibility?

"As far as I'm concerned, in no way," Sadisa replied, turning to his wife.

The latter shook her head.

"To me she did not say anything either. On my side I did not suspect anything. Perhaps I was influenced by the fact that we have not had any family that has been visiting us for several moons. So I imagined that nothing would happen for a long time."

"That is why this situation is even more intriguing, the youngest of the parents, father Ebata, said. "Did not these people hear about the reputation that was given to our daughter? Or do they simply not care? I find that very strange. Either this young man who is interested in our daughter is a saint, or he is an opportunist. Or else, I no longer understand human beings."

"Let us not be influenced by the context and let this family come," Yinda said. "Let it come forward and we will judge with knowledge. We must also give ourselves time to consult with the guardians of collective memory. They will certainly be able to tell us more. The fact that they come from afar will give us time to know enough."

"They come from so far away that I wonder if the guardians of the collective memory will know enough about them. Perhaps we should consult some who are closer to their land?"

Old Yinda thought for a moment, then decided to conclude.

"All this will be done on time. In the meantime, is there anyone who formally opposes this request?"

There were no negative responses.

"If there is a valid reason to oppose it, apart from what Nsona decides, we will know."

"All right, Sadissa. So here is what I suggest..."

Moments later, they were all back in front of the visitors. Old Yinda got up to speak again.

"First of all, forgive us for taking for so long. But we have some good news for you. No one on principle opposes your child's willingness to marry ours, subject to his feeling. But we reserve the possibility to make a final decision once we know more about your family. I think you understand that."

A nod answered old Yinda's words.

"But beyond our decision as parents, the dean of the family continued, we have a custom in our family to leave the last word to the main person involved. We will therefore decide as a last resort, but not without having heard her beforehand. To do this, of course, she will have to see your child as well. Thank you."

He sat back.

"We understand and respect what you said," the spokeswoman replied. "But our son told us that your child already knows him. They saw each other and talked. I do not think there should be a problem. Since on the principle there is no opposition, what do you think of bringing our child so that he can express himself? Thank you."

Sitting discreetly in her wicker seat, behind everyone, ma Kimani widened her eyes. The situation was, once again, unprecedented. Obviously, this delegation had prepared well for its arrival. They wanted to be quick. Or was it the son who wanted to go fast and pushed his people to act so? There were all reasons to believe that it was the case. So who was this son who could have such power? He would have already met Nsona, they said. Why did she not tell her anything when she was always confiding in her? Moreover, where was she?"

"We do not mind about that," old Yinda replied. "Still, we shall not decide anything without hearing from our daughter. Whether they have met or not does not change the situation. Now, we are ready to listen to your child. Thank you."

A little floating moment followed, as if the guests themselves were surprised that this request was accepted. Then, after a brief conversation, two of them quickly slipped away.

On her side, ma Kimani had asked that Nsona join them discreetly. In the diffuse brilliance of the torches that had been placed here and there, it would not be difficult. She asked two young girls in the family to go look for her. As it was late, she certainly was not too far away. It would be enough to make a quick tour of the neighbors she used to frequent. This was a very special evening. Everything seemed to have to be done in a hurry. Moments later, she saw the two visitors who had gone to fetch the young man come back.

He followed them very closely. In the light of the torches, she distinguished a very young man. He was tall and looked strong, but he was very young. How could he have such a great influence on people as mature as his companions seemed to be? Moreover, his robe suggested that he was of high social rank, like all those who accompanied him. A sleeveless silk tunic in gold embroidered with gold covered it up to mid-thigh. It was held at the waist by a belt of bronze rings. He wore broad trousers of the same fabric down to the top of the ankles, revealing braided black leather sandals. His forearms were adorned with large bronze bracelets, while a wide necklace, almost like a small metal cape, surrounded his neck and almost covered his shoulders. He was moving forward with the assurance of those who know what they want and above all who they are. Yet no arrogance or pride emanated from him. He just seemed proud to be who he was. He was also quite attractive.

But then she saw his eyes more accurately and felt a strange sensation. They contrasted a little with the rather noble impression he gave off. They seemed to have no expression. Yet he had a smile on his face. She immediately understood that this man, whoever he might be, was not really what he claimed to be. She had the unpleasant feeling of seeing a man playing a role for a reason she did not know. He was trying to be what he was not. She was convinced of that. But for what reason? Why not be oneself when one comes to propose for a marriage? What could he have to hide? Suddenly she knew that her daughter should not marry this man, whoever he was. Fortunately, the final decision would not be made right away. She would have time to talk to the family and especially to Nsona.

The young man had just sat down and the spokeswoman was ready to resume her intervention. All the attention was on her. She turned to the newcomer.

"Will you get up, please," she said. "Come close to me, my child."

Then she turned towards her interlocutors.

"Here is our son who brought us here. As you can certainly see, he is still very young, but we can assure you that he is quite mature. But I am going to let him present and talk to you himself."

She sat down and left the young man standing. The latter seemed tense. He let his gaze wander as if he were looking for someone and for good reason, Nsona was still not there.

"Mothers and fathers, all my greetings to you," he began, bowing his head slightly.

He paused, feeling that all were hanged to his lips.

"Well, this situation that I started now seems so important to me that I am now a little apprehensive."

grandfathers say, "one cannot shave someone's head in his absence"."

He turned to his family to find out what was going on in the search for Nsona's whereabouts. But there was no echo of his presence in the neighborhood.

"You said you were ready to go back," he said. "You will have to wait for our response or postpone this matter until much later, given where you come from. What do you say? Thank you."

He sat down. A discreet conversation began in the group of visitors. The tone seemed to rise gradually. Suddenly, the spokeswoman stood up.

"Forgive us, we need to talk to each other to know what we are going to do. Let us withdraw for a moment. Thank you."

Before Yinda's acquiescence they retreated to the side of the house to reach a conclusion. Ma Kimani chose this moment to talk to her husband.

"Tell me, pa Sadisa, have you noticed, as I did, that this young boy has undeniable power over all these people? You could even think they are not his family. It is amazing, is it not?"

Pa Sadisa looked at her. He seemed surprised.

"No, not really. But I may not have been paying attention. I shall take a closer look at how they behave."

"Moreover, he does not seem very friendly despite his smile."

"However, he spoke very well earlier."

"Maybe too well. I look forward to hearing Nsona about it. I am surprised that if they have ever reached a point where this young man comes here with such confidence, she has not told me. I find it all very strange. And where is she, anyway?"

At that very moment, some girls were coming back from their research. Ma Kimani was quick to question them.

"So, have you any news about your sister? Where is she?"

"We do not know," one of them replied. "We went around the neighbors but no one has seen her tonight."

The visitors came back to their places to resume the conversation. Each one stayed on his seat for the rest of the encounter. Once everyone was ready, the spokeswoman talked again.

"Forgive us for keeping you waiting. We found a solution. In fact, Tembo wants to tell you himself. He cares. Thank you."

She sat down as the young man stood up.

"Dear family, it is true that the situation is rather special, that is why it seems to me that I must take my responsibilities and speak frankly to you."

He took a deep breath before resuming.

"I do not imagine going back home without Nsona. It will be too difficult for me to go home with the uncertainty of the response. Please do not get me wrong. I am not trying to put you under pressure to make you decide in a hurry. I am trying to make it clear that I have decided to stay here in Mbanza Miongo for as long as it takes you to make your decision. Whether it is one, two, or three moons, I shall wait."

He paused, then went on.

"I also do not want you to believe that with Nsona we have agreed on a common future, no. I can even assure you that she does not know that I was supposed to run tonight. As proof, she is not here. Maybe she will not appreciate my approach, but I think you will agree with me, if I do not make that decision, no one will make it for me; and certainly not her. With all that is currently burdening her, it would be a new burden for her because, as you know, in our customs it is men who make the move. On the contrary, if I have made this decision, it is also to show her that despite everything, she is still coveted. And if some people no longer dare to show up for her for fear of having to face the gaze of others, I think your child is worth confronting them. And my intention is to give her a life that will allow her to become herself again and above all to remain herself and live happily ever after. I hope I have been understood and that my decision to stay will allow you to take your time to give your answer. Thank you."

He sat back in a revealing silence of the disturbance he had created by his words. A few murmurs took place on both sides for a few moments. Then old Yinda spoke again.

"Forgive us, we must once again talk to this new situation. Thank you."

The group headed back to the house. This time, when they gathered, there was a silence. Obviously some who were categorically against in the first conciliabule had evolved in their point of view. The young man's words had apparently touched hearts. Old Yinda felt it. This young man was very skilful. His first words were for father Sadisa.

"What do you think of this young man's words, brother? And I ask you too, Kimani because I have the feeling that some of us here are ready to support this boy's request."

"He spoke very well, indeed," Sadisa replied. "But should we be seduced by simple beautiful words? What is really behind this? We do not know."

He turned an interrogative glance at his wife.

"As far as I am concerned, my husband knows my position, I have a negative feeling about this boy from the beginning. For all his fine words, I will not change my mind. My opinion is made. And I will do everything I can to get our child to follow it."

"So we have your opinion," replied old Yinda. "What do the others think?"

The others had mixed opinions. Some had indeed been seduced by the young man's words and made it known, arguing that Nsona was in a situation that would cause her to no longer dismiss any suitors because a reputation is difficult to undo. The young man was visibly guided by very noble motives. It was therefore better to seize this unexpected opportunity and thus close this whole story. It would even be best to respond immediately by telling him that he was accepted into the family and thus avoiding long waiting days for an answer that might be to his disadvantage. To which the dean of the clan answered bluntly that it would certainly not be.

"May I remind you that Nsona is not here," he recalled, "and that the last word belongs to her as is customary in our family. So let us be serious! We will make the same answer, which is that the answer will come in a timely manner, while praising this boy's approach. Let us wrap up this evening. I am getting tired. And where is Nsona?"

Moments later, the message had passed. What a surprise to see a whole set of gifts arrive from Tembo to thank them, he said, for having received them despite the late hour and the sudden nature of their visit. The young man offered pieces of noble cloth for Nsona's mother as well as for her aunts and sisters. He also offered presents for his father and uncles, precious metal objects and also prestigious fabrics. All this was supplemented by three sheep and a young zebu in excellent shape which he asked to be consumed in his honor.

Incredulous and reluctant at first, the Sadisa clan eventually accepted the offerings. The argument that convinced everyone was that it would not be appropriate to disappoint or discourage or even frustrate a young man who showed such good will. If the answer were to be unfavorable to him in the end, it would make him two refusals which could lead to a huge disillusionment which he would not deserve given his noble approach.

Father Sadisa let himself be persuaded. Unlike ma Kimani; who made it known. She had the feeling that the young man was buying his daughter. She had no idea how right she was and how much this open demonstration of her opinion would cost her.

*

Nsona came back home very late that night. She waited until everyone was in bed. She was tired of seeing at home all the people she considered to be at her bedside. She could not stand it anymore. Of course, it was with laudable intentions and she was still grateful, but she could not stand to keep smiling to show that she was fine.

She returned discreetly with the complicity of some of her sisters, who had found her at a neighbor's house earlier but had decided, at her request, to say not to have seen her. There was always a strong complicity between the children towards the parents, the children of the Sadisa clan being particularly strong. Not in the mood to deal with the situation that night, she preferred to stay away and let her family manage the situation. She trusted them. She would agree with their decision.

4

"Do not you marry this young man, do you hear? Ooh, it hurts so! God, it is so painful!! Ohhh!..."

Nsona held her mother's hand as she lay on her diaper. She did not understand what was going on. Ma Kimani had collapsed in the courtyard, holding her chest again as it had happened to her before. But this time, the pain had been such that she could not bear it. In addition to the pain, frequent bouts of coughing shook her violently. This had never happened to her before.

It had now been several days since Tembo and his family had come to introduce themselves. Nsona's relatives had also remained on site in order to conclude the situation as soon as possible. Discussions about the future of Nsona were bitter throughout these passing days. She kept coming back into all discussions, whether she was there or not. The strong tendency was to push her into the arms of the suitor. As for mother Kimani, she had gradually begun to change the point of view of some. Little by little, she was able to impose her refusal of this union. In her argumentation, she spoke of the difficulties that the guardians of memory had in gathering information about the clan of the young Tembo.

Indeed, it usually only took a few days to have some essential information about a family even living at the other end of the territory. People often questioned on how these men were able to communicate and transmit information so quickly. But this time, nothing came to enlighten old Yinda and his family about Tembo's origins and family past. This was surprising and added more and more credit to mother Kimani's point of view. Moreover, being the young woman's mother, it was necessary to consider her intuition. After all, a mother is a mother and is the one who knows best what is good for her child. A mother's intuition is often the best, if not always. Moreover, she had made her opinion from the beginning and had not changed even once while her husband had been more uncertain.

The most surprising thing was finally Nsona's attitude. She, who had always been sure of her fact with regard to her marital future, had abandoned herself to the family's decision this time. This had destabilized more than one. In the end, most had concluded that this meant an acceptation. Or else, she would have clearly expressed her opposition. Was not that clear enough?

It was in these circumstances that ma Kimani had to convince both of them, the uncertainty displayed by her daughter did not help her in any way. She still managed it very slowly, but at the cost of a psychological effort that had visibly exhausted her. Especially since Nsona herself, for once, did not seem to object to the situation. This was something new. So many had wanted to marry her, and now she was ready to unite with a man whom no one knew anything about. Even worse, on whom the guardians of the collective memory could not know much.

"Why are you telling me that? Think about your health, instead of thinking about me."

Nsona did not understand the situation, while everyone was busy around her mother. A healer had been called to come to her bedside and he still had not arrived. Why did it take him so long? Not far from her, father Sadisa was prostrated, but she did not see him. She did not see what condition he was in. If she had seen it, she would have understood. The poor man had been in this situation before. It was a long time ago, when he was still a young boy no older than she was herself today. He had had the bad experience of seeing his mother collapse just like his wife. He knew only too well what had happened afterwards. He had seen the healer that his father had called. As the man had been helpless, he had seen another one arrive. It was only when he had seen a great, feared and reputed sorcerer arrive that he had understood that his father was desperate, distraught and that he had lost all lucidity. If he had been himself, he would never have appealed to this kind of character who profited more from the plight of those who called upon him than he was really effective. The rest had shown it well.

There was a bustle at the entrance to the house. A woman from the clan approached father Sadisa.

"Father Sadisa, the healer is here," she said.

"The healer? What for? Why not a wizard too?" he was outraged.

The woman, surprised, withdrew without further insistence. She felt that she should not disturb him any longer. Old Yinda had to intervene with the desperate husband.

"Please, Sadisa," he begged him. "Think about her and let the healer treat her. I know what is overwhelming you. I too still have those pictures in my mind and yet they are a long way back. But we are in a different era and things change. Let the healer intervene."

Father Sadisa did not answer. He merely turned his heels silently and went outside. He did not want to attend an intervention that he knew was doomed to failure. Moments later, the healer hurriedly left, admitting his helplessness at the sight of what he described as unnatural.

"It is always so," father Sadisa exclaimed bitterly. "When they are helpless, they say it is not natural. A bunch of incompetents and charlatans! That is what these people are!"

No one dared contradict him. Within a few moons, he had the feeling that his life was falling apart. Since the appeal in the street, of which he had been the target, all the quietness and happiness he had known for so long seemed to fade away. He even seemed to notice that his clientele was fading. Was all this simply due to the consequences of his daughter's attitude, which himself considered legitimate, towards all her suitors? It was true that she had rebuffed a very large number of requests, a number that had never been seen, but was that a reason enough to make her responsible for the misfortunes of both? What an injustice. But he did not blame his daughter. He would never blame her.

Sitting on a bench in the courtyard, he watched the few visitors who had learned on his wife's sudden health deterioration. He read on the faces the resignation of those who knew that the situation was irreversible. Some were already confirming this by coming to shake his hands in an anticipated gesture of compassion.

*

"Tell me you will not marry this young man, tell me."

If Nsona had been in a psychological state that would have allowed her to understand what was really going on around her, she would have responded immediately to her mother. Instead, she hesitated for a few moments, not understanding why she insisted so much on making him promise not to marry Tembo. Why so much obstinacy? What did she know about him that no one else knew or could not suspect? Was it simply the intuition of a mother guided by the love she had for her daughter? She closed her eyes and lowered her head, feeling a slight vertigo. Fortunately, she was sitting, otherwise she would have probably collapsed, exhausted both physically and psychologically.

Nsona did not realize how long she remained so. She felt a caress on her hand, which relieved her. She opened her eyes, deciding to answer to her mother what she wanted to hear. She then realized that it was not a caress she had felt, but the friction of the white loincloth that had just been placed on her mother's remains. Someone had just taken her by the shoulders and comforted her, without saying anything. It was father Sadisa. Their lives were about to change and he had to show her that she was not suffering on her own.

*

Mother Kimani's funeral took place the next afternoon, as usual. Unlike recent times when many people did not come to visit him because of the rumors about Nsona, there was a crowd of visitors who came to pay tribute to her remains. But she no longer had the ability to see them, even though she had gone feeling rather abandoned. This made father Sadisa even bitter and sad. He had always thought that people needed support and marks of consideration when they are alive. After their death, it serves only the living to give themselves good conscience and a good image in relation to each other.

Among all those who had come to pay tribute to the deceased, a visitor was particularly noticed by his omnipresence or rather that of his relatives. He was first at the side of father Sadisa through his relatives, who were a constant moral and material support by offering their help in the organization and by demonstrating in this matter a remarkable efficiency. It was as if they had always done that all their life. In any case, people were unanimous. As for the visitor himself for whom they were there, he was on his side very present with the young woman. This visitor, who was none other than Tembo, had been able to be accepted, even adopted, by the women of the family. Beyond the gifts he had offered on his very first visit, he showed fully marital presence and tenderness to Nsona who needed it. Everyone had noticed it and everyone appreciated it.

Imperceptibly, without anyone noticing, the work mother Kimani had done to convince her loved ones not to see Nsona marry this new suitor was fading. The young man was in fact running a real campaign of closeness with the family. Chance had no place in his approach. Yet, seen from away, he seemed disinterested on his side, even though one knew the action he had undertaken. His presence was such that a few days after the funeral, when he had withdrawn to let Nsona's family recover from its emotions, his absence was felt.

When he returned almost a moon later, he was greeted with great sympathy by father Sadisa. He welcomed him with all honors due to an important figure. He realized that. He was not surprised when Nsona's father told him what he had been waiting for.

"Listen, son. You have been here for a long time and you have been waiting for a sign from us. I know you might get impatient. Also, I spoke with Nsona and the whole family. We are ready to receive you and your family to end your wait. So you can finally go home. I shall talk to your people."

*

The guardians of the collective memory had finally provided information about Tembo's family. Almost non-existent at first, these had flowed surprisingly afterwards. While the networks of these eminent members of the community were quite dense and, above all, very effective, the sudden abundance of information was unusual. But it had not moved anyone, blinded that everyone was by the will to please this boy so kind, so generous, and so devoted.

Everyone had actually heard what he wanted to hear. Tembo's family was a respected old family? Good. Tembo's family came from a clan close to the imperial family? Very well. Tembo himself was a respectful and hardworking boy? What more could be asked for? Above all, Nsona herself was not against this union, despite the opposition of her late mother. Moreover, the latter had not had this latest information from the guardians of the collective memory. Otherwise, she would undoubtedly have changed her mind. All were convinced that her objections were only because of her ignorance of this information. They completely forgot that mother Kimani had raised her objections not because of a lack of information about the young man's family or clan, but because of the unpleasant impression she had had the first time she had seen him at her home. Was she right? Was she wrong? Only the future would tell. In any case, today her word had no consideration, especially since she was no longer there to defend it. Not her, not anyone. Not even father Sadisa.

It was therefore agreed that the two families would meet a moon later, so that as many members of the two clans as possible would be able to attend the ceremonies. It would be a great wedding because it was long overdue. Nsona was so beautiful that she should have found a husband a long time ago. But her demands had made the deadline arrive only now. This young woman, who used to refuse up to a dozen marriage proposals per moon, had been left without a single proposal for a very long time at a point that some had come to wonder whether she had not cursed herself. And now, after all these adventures and especially after the death of her mother, an unexpected party came to her. From what he showed, he was very wealthy and had a good family. Everything a young woman could hope for. Was not that strange? A local belief was that in certain circumstances there were people who had the ability, even in spite of themselves, to attract the good graces of geniuses and to get even what they no longer hoped for. All they had to do was to desire something very hard, this wish was captured by a genius who would go through it and grant it, thus allowing himself a right. The right to take a life in the person's entourage. So, certainly that the brutal death of ma Kimani was the consequence of Nsona's wish to find such a good party. Since she had started misleading the suitors, it was not surprising. Poor ma Kimani.

Many were therefore convinced of Nsona's responsibility in her mother's death. The most convinced were jealous women who could not admit that she could achieve all this happiness simply by her beauty and personality. She had necessarily sold her soul or worse, that of an innocent. It was not possible otherwise. But these women were not yet at the end of their resentment. They would still have to endure the lavish wedding that would follow. Especially since it would take place in the main square of the neighborhood and the groom-to-be had decreed that anyone who would like to participate would be welcome. There would be enough to eat and drink for everyone, without exception. A nice plan for a banquet.

*

The waiting period ran very quickly. Yet each family had time to prepare as best as possible. Tembo's family had inherited the most important workload. It had to make sure, as their son had wanted, that everyone would not lack anything. As for Nsona's family, they would take care of the families and their closest guests. This was already a good prospect given the high number of individuals in the families alone. The particular context of this union also made it absolutely necessary for these ceremonies to be a success. At first the main one; which would take place in the big square. So everyone could attend, as wished by the future husband. It would last all night after the union was pronounced. But there would also be the final reception of the bride's family at the bride's home the next day. Meanwhile, there would still be festivities in the main square, on which the spouses would make a quick appearance to honor the guests.

Preparations began logically several days before the wedding. But the result was only visible when the day came, as if everything had been hidden nobody knew where. Groups of musicians and dancers that no one had ever seen came to mingle with the traditional local artists who were invited for this type of situation. Even the master of ceremonies was not one of those who generally officiated in the agglomeration. All were known. When it was not this one, it was another. And yet this man was leading the debates as if he had always been a child of the country. His volubility and mastery of the organization in accordance with custom would seduce the guests. He knew how to place each person without ever being wrong. He knew how to talk to everyone as if he knew everything about them. Who was this man who seemed to take his role, his profession, so seriously? Faced with so much talent, the question did not arise for long. Moreover, the various festivities answered the questions of the most curious. It was concluded that he was certainly coming from the land of Tembo. That was not wrong.

Singers, musicians and dancers had invaded the alleys in the neighborhood. It was still daylight and they had not yet started to deploy all their skills. This would happen when the wedding ceremony would take place. It was already the middle of the afternoon and the atmosphere was starting to get more and more electric. Everyone chose the best possible location so as not to miss any crumbs of the festivities. The eagerness to see the one who had managed to get Nsona's hand was palpable. One had to see it. What was so exceptional about him that he could succeed in seducing her when so many others had failed? Certainly, he had to be a man of an exceptional quality. But there came the jealousy of the men, who felt that he had nothing out of the ordinary. He had simply taken advantage of a difficult situation of a young woman to make her bend. After all, it was not so honorable.

Suddenly the song that announced the arrival of the future husband recanted. Indeed, a procession was coming step by step. A dozen of athletic fellows carried wooden seats that rested on logs. The seat was covered with flamboyant silk fabrics whose radiance was accentuated by the sun rays. The bright colors contrasted with the slightly darker outfit worn by Tembo, who was sitting on the seat. He wore a long light brown sleeveless tunic. An unusual color for a wedding, some said, but why not? The tunic was held at the waist by a gold belt. His bare arms were covered with large bracelets of the same precious metal. His feet were hidden by the many fabrics that covered the seat. A dark gown went up over his shoulder and fell back onto his back. When gazes were on his face, they discovered a rather youthful man, almost a teenager, but with an indefinable, impenetrable look, which contrasted with his features that made him look very young. But was not his future wife herself a very young woman? Tembo had a furnished black hair that showed that he took great care of it. In fact, they shone slightly, suggesting that oil had been applied to them. A gold ring surrounded them, representing the head of a kind of animal that the audience had difficulty identifying. But they quickly moved on, taking up in heart the welcome song that had spread to the alleys around, even among those who did not see the procession. The atmosphere was such that everyone was carried away by the surrounding enthusiasm.

A group of excited children followed the future husband noisily, at a rather respectable distance from the carried seat. They did not dare get closer because an intimidating number of guards made sure they stayed away. It had to be so, because the procession did not stop at the groom's seat alone. Behind him came a column of carriers who had on their shoulders or on their heads what could be guessed as gifts for the bride's family. Further on, a troupe of dancers followed, which could be easily guessed by their outfits and dances that they were not from the surroundings. Their choreographies were indeed rather leaping, far from the characteristic swaying movements of the traditional dances of the region. Yet, although barely discovering the style, many of the spectators along the route were already trying. And many did so with obvious success, provoking the smiles of the dancers who encouraged them to do even more by setting an example for them. Some of them wore shiny wooden masks that represented various figures of the forest or the savannah. The rest of their outfit consisted of simple skirts with linen fringes and raffia over short silk trousers. Three rows of musicians followed with various instruments. These included shekeres, sanzas and gongobas. All these artists filled the atmosphere with sound waves produced by the dexterity of their fingers on their instruments. But the most important characters, beyond the bride and groom, were already settled in the square. The most influential members of each family were placed in two rows face to face. At the end of these rows, facing the central aisle that had been freed, two beautiful carved precious wooden seats inlaid with gold were placed. They had been manufactured for the occasion. The bride and groom would come to seat on them at the end of the ceremony. While waiting for this moment, everyone could admire the reflections of the sun that emanated from the gold inlays and precious fabrics that covered them.

Tembo had just arrived among his family and sat comfortably in a seat that looked very likely as those planned for the future spouses. He had a shy and reserved attitude that contrasted with the barely concealed elegance of his outfit. His gaze, impenetrable as mother Kimani had noticed, roamed the audience with slowness and distance that was almost arrogance. And yet, the feeling he inspired was rather close to sympathy. This was certainly due to his youthful appearance.

Suddenly there was silence. The master of ceremonies had spoken with the spokesmen of both parties and had given way to the representative of the coveted family. The latter advanced between the first two rows occupied by the families.

"Families, good morning to you!" he exclaimed. "We are gathered here for a reason we all know! Well, we think we do! But to confirm this, I invite my counterpart to refresh our memory so that everyone can be sure of the reason for his presence here today."

He withdrew as the opposing spokesman advanced.

"Families, good morning to you!" the latter began. "Indeed, as my counterpart said, we all know why we are here! It is a reason for joy and celebration, as we can all see!"

He showed the audience with a circular gesture of the arm.

"And so it is with great pleasure that I will repeat this purpose that unites us here!"

He summarized the situation, modestly ignoring the bride's difficulties. He related the two lovers' encounter, concluding that the young man had decided from the first day that this young woman would be his wife no matter what. He insisted on the last words. This elicited a murmur of admiration in the audience. Here is a man who knew what he wanted and thus came to his ends. Surely he would be a dignified man and would take good care of his wife. Nsona was lucky after all. This marriage would restore her serenity and make her forget very quickly the recent bad periods of her life. After having sent off all these contenders, and sometimes not the least interesting, she had still managed to get the best possible party. Many of the women in the audience were in a wave of jealousy. They would have liked to be in her shoes. But she was in place and she strongly was.

After the traditional introductory words of the ceremony, the interminable but equally exciting period of handing out presents to the bride's parents and family began. Thus, the audience saw the appearance of the most impressive pieces of cloth that were normally intended for the bride's mother, but which were eventually offered to the dean of the clan. Other pieces were for the other women. There were sets for the father and the other men. There were impressive necklaces and other precious metal bracelets. Everyone found their own way. Finally, the traditional cattle marched, forming a procession that seemed never to have an end. Was this young woman really worth all this wealth exposure? If her suitor thought so, then it was because she was worth it. He also wanted to inflict a fateful blow on all the rumors that had smeared the young woman for too long. An indisputable proof of love.

Once the presents were handed over to the bride-to-be's family, time came for her to arrive. She arrived on foot, escorted by her closest sisters, but particularly with her best friend, Lukuayi, right by her side. Nsona paid tribute to her mother by wearing only fabric from her production. She sported a tight, brightly colored dress that stopped at the knees, but covered the rest of her legs with fiery color. The top of the dress was stopped above the breasts by a sky blue stripe that accentuated the colors of the lower part. A cape attached to it covered the upper arms. It was sky blue and lined with the fabric that made up the bulk of the dress. Her neck and shoulders were almost covered by a necklace with multiple rows of bronze pieces. A gift that his father had wanted to give her for this very special occasion. He had put a large part of his personal fortune in it. Who would it have served for if not her only daughter? She was really the only one he had, even though there was the clan. The young woman's hair was a work of art. It had been enhanced in such a way that it could only have been done by specialized hands. They were bright and dotted with a reddish earth reminiscent of the bright colors of her dress. The braids that formed it were of impressive regularity. They formed a spiral and ended in a cone held together by a beautiful and wide bronze ring. She had all of a princess. But was she not the princess of the day?

At her sight, the audience's first reaction was a silence of wonder. Then, gradually, murmurs began to rise before ending in a traditional song that praised the beauty of the bride. It was sung by all. Both the assistance and the family of the future wife; but also by the family of the future spouse. That was very unusual. Generally, the visiting family stayed on the reserve. But this marriage was really not meant to be like any other. It was out of the ordinary by its location, by the number of people, the genre and the quality of the gifts offered, but also by the attitude of each other, particularly the future step family which showed an unusual familiarity and enthusiasm. They seemed eager to be accepted, even appreciated not only by their counterparts, but also by the population. It was true that coming from another country, it could have been a reason to encounter some mistrust, but obviously this time it had no impact.

Nsona was approaching the corridor between the two rows of families. Gradually, some voices abandoned the song to launch some obvious observation.

"You are the most beautiful, Nsona!!" A first one cried out.

"Nsona! You are a worthy daughter of Mbanza Miongo!!" another one yelled.

"We are proud of you, my sister!!" Another one continued after.

Soon there were as many voices giving compliments to the young woman as there were voices singing. However, they all accompanied her until her escort installed her in one of the seats provided for this purpose. The master of ceremonies moved back to the centre of the corridor. The silence came back gradually, of course.

"My friends, we are now heading towards the moment you have all been waiting for! That we are all waiting for! I will make way for the spokesperson of this young woman whom you have all just cheered so that the rest will go on as usual."

He strayed. Another rather old man took his place. He addressed the young woman directly with a loud voice that carried far beyond the ears of the families around him.

"Nsona, my child! See all the people who are here for you! Everybody! But there is someone here who made everyone come here! Someone who showed up to ask for your hand. He told us you know him! Everything has already been said, everything has already been done between the two families! All that is missing is your assent! All that is missing is your confirmation! So are you going to make everyone happy or are you going to make this moment a moment of disappointment and shame?"

He was silent for a brief moment, showing the assistance of the hand.

"See, Nsona! See everyone, my child! They are all hanging at your lips and at your decision!!"

As he went to invite her to speak, a powerful voice rose languidly on the side of the young bride's family. The voice evoked the joy of seeing the young woman finally find her soul mate. It vibrated with an unfeigned emotion. Such that other voices joined it to express the same feeling of happiness. That voice was Lukuayi's. She was certainly the happiest of the women who attended the ceremony. She had hoped so much for her friend that she was convinced that it was God who had fulfilled her desires. It could not have been any other way. The song evoked the happiness of the event, attributed to the almighty. She also thanked the ancestors. The improvised chorus lasted for a long time, but no one wanted it to stop despite the impatience that everyone had to see Nsona heading towards her future husband. For it was certain that she would accept. At last she was going to be able to start a home. At the end of the song, the young woman exchanged an accomplice and tender look with her friend. Silence was made again when all eyes were inevitably on Nsona.

The young woman was standing upright despite a little shyness in her eyes. She spoke.

"Good morning to everyone, to all the families and to everyone who is here. Thank you all for being here."

The voice was soft and firm at the same time. This contrasted with the shyness that emanated from her gaze. Silence was such that it could be heard far enough away.

"Indeed, I was well informed of the arrival of a young man some moons ago who claimed to have met me and I can tell you that if I am here it is because he told the truth."

There were applause and cries of joy. She had spoken all in one breath, as if she had been afraid of being interrupted. But at such a moment, no one would have dared interrupt her. The awaiting was too great to finally see this young woman commit. She who had repelled so many suitors; she who had apparently provoked so much animosity, at last she would be engaged.

"Well, my child," the spokesman exclaimed. "You just have to designate him to us so that we can all be sure that we are talking about the same young man!"

Nsona slowly descended the corridor through which she had come, letting her gaze wander on either side. She pretended not to find the one she was looking for. She then went back before letting a broad smile crack her face. She then snuck between the guests and stopped right before Tembo.

"He is the one!" she said with a big smile.

"So come over here, my children!" the spokesman ordered." Come on, so everyone can see you. What a lovely couple!! Is it not?"

He had appealed the assistance. New cries and cheers rang out in the surrounding alleys. Even those who did not see the scene let themselves be carried away by enthusiasm and joined the cheers. The two young people took their place in both seats. Everything then went awry. Two women brought the traditional cup of palm wine that the stars of the day each drank in turn until emptying it, as a sign of mutual commitment. Nsona then appeared before her father with a new glass of wine. She knelt before him and handed it to him.

"Papa," she said. "Please, do drink this cup as an offering for agreeing to grant my hand."

Father Sadisa stood up in his seat. He looked at his daughter straight in the eye.

"My child, I am glad that this moment has finally arrived for you, for us. I am just sorry it is a little late."

He paused, retaining a sob. Nsona, who had looked down, raised her head and comforted him with her eyes.

"But God decided so. So let us accept it and move forward."

He recovered completely.

"So you are telling us that you know this boy and that you are ready to commit?"

"Yes, papa."

"Are you sure of yourself? You are doing this on your own free will, without any constraints? Is that your choice?"

"Yes, papa."

"So I can drink this cup without fear; you will always honor your family as a wife; you will respect your husband, your new family and you will never be a disgrace to us?"

"Yes, papa. You can drink without fear."

Father Sadisa stood up so that as many people as possible could see and hear him.

"So, before all here, before our ancestors and before God, I affirm that it is with great joy, pleasure and without any ulterior motives that I will empty this cup."

The act followed the words and he slowly drank the cup of palm wine until he emptied it of its last drop. Then he hugged his daughter for a long time. He saw his whole life go by. He knew that Nsona was going to leave and for the first time since long they would not see each other every day. He thought of his beloved wife who would never live this moment. He recalled that she had opposed it in her lifetime and that if she had not died so suddenly, this ceremony might never have taken place. Deep down, he asked mother Kimani for her forgiveness and hoped not to have to regret this decision contrary to the wishes of his late wife. He prayed briefly that the new era that opened to his daughter would be a continuation of joy and happiness. He took the young woman back to her seat and put her hand in her husband's.

"Tembo, son of Weya and Mawa, you came on your own to ask for this young woman's hand. We happily grant it to you. Nsona just needs to be happy; and she will make you happy. We are entrusting her to you. Take care of her."

Tembo should have taken his wife's hand without reacting. He should not have said anything until a person from his parents spoke and also confirmed his choice. It was customary in his land. But he went over and spoke. No one in the area realized that he was breaking a rule of his house. No one knew the traditional rules in Songo or Mbuila. Oddly enough, among Tembo's family no one reacted. Maybe mother Kimani would have noticed something. Who knew?

"Father Sadisa, it is with great emotion that I take on this responsibility that is mine to look after your child. I am committed to doing so with all my will and my heart. I assure you that you can be confident about my commitment."

The crowd began to cheer the spouses, covering the young man's voice. The essentials were done and Nsona was married. Finally! What else was there to look forward to? Festivities and dinner. This is what all minds were now turned to.

5

After the wedding ceremony, night would certainly be long. Tembo promised food for everyone and he was going to keep his word. The bride and groom had left the guests but returned later after having changed their outfits. Nsona had chosen a simpler outfit made of a wide sky-blue dress that accentuated her shapes much less than the one in the afternoon. As for her husband, he had changed his outfit to a wide tunic too, but the colors kept the same dark trend. But no one was formal. This was certainly due to the customs of his country.

Musical groups had invaded the square and the surrounding alleyways. There were stalls all over the place run by waiters and waitresses from no one knew where. These stalls presented appetizing dishes and the guests, whether they were from the family or not, feasted. Yet, despite the crowds, the meals never seemed to dry up. As shares were served, other ones arrived as if by magic, feeding the endless stalls. Tembo kept his word. Everything seemed so well organized that it did not seem like anything could go wrong. There were sort of guards that ensured that nothing degenerated between the participants by intervening at the slightest snag. They were so quick to intervene that they seemed to anticipate what was going to happen. The alleys were unusually busy. A careful eye might even have noticed that in addition to waitresses, waiters and other security guards, there were many unknown faces in the area. But the enthusiasm generated by the celebratory situation was such that everyone spoke to everyone without asking any questions. Moreover, the carelessness generated by a few sips of good fermented drinks was certainly not going to help to remain lucid.

In the main square, the families had also become more acquainted. The elders of each clan had come together and shared some distant memories of their youth. They exchanged on their life experience. They narrated the evolution and family constitutions of their respective clans. However, there were some areas of vagueness in the accounts that the dean of Tembo's family made. This could happen because memory is not always reliable. It could also happen that we did not know everything about all of our own. Yet, for his part, old Yinda mastered everything about his own perfectly. From the oldest member of the clan to the youngest, he was able to evoke each of the routes as well as that of their parents, grandparents and great-grandparents. Old Yinda was a true patriarch who loved his own. He was truly exceptional. He was the cement of the clan and he made sure to pass on his knowledge to the youngest. He could have been a custodian of collective memory because he was so gifted. But he had chosen a different path and he used his memory skill only for his family. And it was very useful as in these moments of exchange and conviviality between two families, two clans that united and where one had to present their own to their in-laws. The debates were therefore somewhat unbalanced. But did it really matter? Over time each would learn to know the other better. There was no hurry.

The two newlyweds had hosted the parade of guests who had congratulated them for long moments. Dishes were then served to them and they enjoyed a little of each one presented to them. The dishes were paraded and they were each better than the other. Nsona, who had an appetite well above average, held back with each pass of dish to feed. She wondered if she would have the opportunity to find all these dishes later. In any case, she hoped so. They talked very little. Did the dishes captivate them so much? Or did they have nothing to say to each other? Was it shyness between these two young men at the point that each was waiting for the other to speak?

"It is really a pity your parents could not make it. They would certainly have appreciated this beautiful ceremony that you offered me."

"I know, but the deadline to come was a little too short. They would have had to travel the route by forced march. That would not have been a good idea."

"It was quite possible to postpone this day, by the time they would have arrived."

"Are you not happy to be married at last?"

"If, of course, but..."

"So forget my parents and enjoy those moments. You will not, I think, have the opportunity to live them again, will you?"

"You are right. This kind of event only happens once."

Tembo had spoken to his wife in a soft but firm voice that had made her understand that he did not wish to dwell on the subject. So she decided not to insist. She would have liked to know more about his parents. But it did not matter; she would have plenty of time to meet them and get to know them. She understood that among those who accompanied her new husband, there was not what could be described as a close relative. There was no uncle on either the father's or the mother's side. There was no aunt. There was no brother or sister. Only a few members of the group who had been portrayed as distant cousins, as well as friends of his parents, constituted his closest relationships. The others were part of his commercial caravan. However, all these people behaved like a real family and honored the groom with their respectful and responsible attitude.

*

Night was already pretty dark. In all the alleys there were spectacular entertainments. There were crowds either around the bands or around the stalls that continued incredibly to present irresistible meals. And above all, there seemed to be even more people than during the day, when many of the inhabitants of the area had decided to return home to enjoy, if it was still possible, the rest of the short night remaining. So where did all these people come from? It was amazing.

The bride and groom had left the main square and had retired for the night. The marriage was effective and the young couple could now spend the night together. But they had separated and had each gone to spend the night in a different place. It was a big break from tradition. Tembo had joined the place where he had spent the last moons waiting for his wedding. As for Nsona, she had simply returned home, to her father's house. Tembo had explained that he did not want them to spend their first night together anywhere other than at their legitimate home in Songo. It was a matter of principle. They had a little trouble understanding him, but they had to deal with it. It was their choice. Well, especially Tembo's.

She was sitting in her room, the one she had grown up in and learned to become an adult. The one in which her mother had come so many times to support her in difficult times, to teach her how society worked, to tell her what she could and could not afford. She had also come to congratulate her on certain occasions when she had honored her family in a way or another. She looked at the walls covered with various decorations and saw her whole childhood parade. She remembered all the time she had spent there, from the first day she had arrived. All the happiness she had experienced here ended so brutally and quickly that she had some difficulty in realizing what was happening. Brutal because of the death of his mother, quick by this marriage so suddenly concluded.

"How do you feel? Are you happy?"

Lukuayi had just entered the room, sporting a big smile. She took her friend in her arms.

"It has all happened so fast! I am not really sure what is going on. I do not know if I should laugh or cry. Everything is getting mixed up in my mind."

Lukuayi sat on the edge of the bed beside Nsona. She guessed and understood the conflicting feelings that animated her friend.

"Yes, I understand," she said."You have just experienced the greatest emotions possible in a very short time. Negative and positive emotions all almost at the same time. But I am sure that over time, all this will fade in your mind. In fact, all of this happened for a specific reason."

"Really? Which one?"

"I do not know. But as you know, nothing ever happens for nothing."

Nsona sighed.

"As you say, nothing ever happens for nothing."

There was a brief silence, which Lukuayi heartedly broke.

"In any case, positive emotions were worth it!"

They laughed softly.

"Oh yes, you can say so," Nsona replied. "What a day!!"

"And above all what an evening!! Do you realize there was food for all those people who were there? How was that possible? He must have a hell of a lot of money, young Tembo. And where did all these people come from? Can you tell me?"

"Definitely acquaintances and acquaintances of Tembo's acquaintances. Some of them had to come from his country and therefore from far away. That is certainly why we knew very few of them."

"All right, Lukuayi conceded. But what about the food? How could they refuel so quickly for so many people? It was really impressive, almost unreal!!"

Nsona tried a semblance of an answer.

"Certainly big money had to be used. And a foolproof organization has allowed such a result."

"If you say so. In any case, I am not about to forget it. Are you leaving for Songo in two days?"

"Yes, we will leave the day after tomorrow at the end of the day. We shall go through your place, so we shall start my journey together? Or are you going to leave later?"

"No, I do not have to do anything here anymore if you leave. You are the one I came for. And then it will be nice to go part of the way together."

They exchanged another smile.

"Our lives have changed so much since we were kids, have they not?" remarked Nsona to her friend.

"Yes, and they will change even more," Lukuayi replied, holding her already bounced belly by her pregnancy.

"How lucky," Nsona said, placing her hand on her friend's belly.

"I am not worried about you. With the handsome young man you have chosen, I am sure that you will soon find yourself in the same condition as I am."

They laughed heartedly again.

"Listen," Nsona recalled, "it is better to go to bed now because tomorrow is going to be another long day."

"Do not forget that you and Tembo will have to go one last time to the big square to honor those who are still celebrating."

A new complicit silence was installed.

"Did you notice?" Lukuayi asked.

"Noticed what?"

Lukuayi had an enigmatic smile.

"Do you remember something you said to me not so long ago? That you were ready to marry the first one who would show up? Well, that is what just happened."

*

At the same time, not far away in the family courtyard, there were still a few family members discussing about this impressive day. The atmosphere of the ceremony was still palpable in the air. The echoes of the festivities were still noticeable. Nearby, some songs could be heard, musical instruments and groups of dancers clearly accompanied by locals. Some were really not ready to give up . A party like this one did not happen every day. And who did they owe it to? To Nsona, of course! As a result, the name of the young woman could sometimes be heard popping up from here and there, paying tribute to her for this beautiful evening and good times. After all, this young woman had been right to be difficult to choose a husband. She had found one who was able to feed almost the entire city. A rich man like none of those known in the area. If she had given in to one of those who had come before him, there was no doubt that she would not have found a better party. How lucky this young woman was. In the end it certainly was not that bad. Perhaps the reputation that had been made to her was not that right. With the few fermented drinks helping, some began to defend her openly by defying anyone who would say evil about her. Ordinary happenings in a night of celebration, in short.

"It is rather extraordinary," old Yinda said.

"What is?" father Ebata asked.

The old man hesitated for a moment.

"Well, a few hours ago, our child was almost a plague, tonight she is almost a queen. Did you hear what some people say out there? Some are willing to fight to defend her."

Father Sadisa sneered discreetly.

"Oh, no wonder, you know. The legendary versatility of the human race. Who knows what they are going to blame her for tomorrow? If the sun does not rise, they will say that it is she who is responsible."

All laughed cheerfully. Old Yinda continued.

"Yes, they will hold her responsible, but then they will thank her because the night will be longer and they will be able to feast even longer!!"

The laughter continued. Then father Sadisa spoke.

"In any case, it is a beautiful day that allows us to see the future in a different way."

There was some sort relief in his voice. There was also a hint of regret. He would have loved his wife to have lived these moments. She who had opposed this young woman so much. She would have deserved it so much and would have been so happy. Finally, perhaps, for he did not forget that she had in her lifetime opposed this union. What could she have seen in this man that he had not noticed?

"Having said that," he said, "I cannot help thinking of my late wife who had opposed this marriage. It is amazing, is it not?"

There was a silence.

"Indeed", old Yinda finally said. "It may be strange that she opposed this young man when all of us were rather excited to see Nsona finally find someone to marry. But it is like everything else. We will only know if it is a good choice over time. No one can know in advance whether a marriage is good or not."

"There is a sure way to make it a success", father Ebata said.

"Wow, yes?" the other two replied in heart.

"Yes, it is to work every day for it to be one."

"You are right! Marriage is an everyday struggle. You have to be vigilant in what you do and say. Particularly in what you say. As the ancestors had said , "the scars of the whip always fade, but those from words never do"."

Old Yinda had spoken in a professorial tone. He suddenly called his wife, a woman in the force of age who was sitting with others a little further away. She was quite younger than her husband but old enough not to make the couple they formed too unbalanced by age.

"Yes, senior. What is going on?"

She had come respectfully closer to the group of men, her legs bent as a sign of respect. Her husband then turned to her.

"Well, I do not know if mother Kimani had had time to do it, although I think she did, but I would rather give you a very important task. A very important one for the future of our child who has just wed."

He pointed his interlocutors with a wave of his hand.

"We were talking just now about how to behave in a home when one is married. Do you want to talk to Nsona and give her the most important advice to remember in her situation? If it is just a reminder, then it will be all the better. As she will leave very quickly, we will have to find a time at the earliest to do this."

Father Sadisa intervened.

"Oh, indeed, yes, eh! Remind her that I drank the wine and that I would not want it to get me choked!"

A new collective laugh rang out.

"And do you realize," old Yinda said, "if you ever have to pay back all that dowry! God help us that day!! And let even the ancestors pray for us!!"

The whole concession had heard his rant and all laughed cheerfully again.

"In any case", his wife concluded, "I will speak to Nsona, even though I know that mother Kimani has done a very good job since the little girl was with her. But a reminder is of no cost. So I shall do it."

"Thank you," father Sadisa concluded.

The sounds of the party still resonated nearby.

"I am still surprised by the crowd that filled the streets today and especially again this night. One wonders where they all come from."

"You know, younger," old Yinda replied when asked by his younger brother, "It should come as no surprise that such a beautiful party attracts people. Would you not like to eat on such an occasion when everything is offered to you? It is just human."

"Since you say so, are you sure that everyone out there is human?"

There was a silence heavy with innuendo. One belief was that at large gatherings, whether in markets or in large ceremonies like this one, some protagonists were just dead people on the return. Dead people in search of a crowd bath that would plunge them back into the world they had left behind. Then they would take advantage of the different opportunities that were presented to them, taking care not to be recognized by relatives or acquaintances from their previous life. This would explain why so many strangers would be present in these moments. Did this silence mean that some people believed it or thought it?

"Come on!" old Yinda exclaimed. "Let us not start rambling. I hope you do not mean it, do you? Anyway, what does it matter? If they are revenants, they will be leaving anyway. Is it not true?"

Father Sadisa tried to regain control.

"I think we should dig a little deeper into the origins of this boy. I keep in mind my poor wife's reluctance to see Nsona make this marriage. So I would like to see the custodian of the collective memory again to find out where they got their information."

"Oh, come on, Sadisa, these people are serious people! They would not have spoken if they did not have reliable information!"

"I know, old Yinda. It is just a matter of reassuring myself. Do you remember the difficulties they had in the beginning to inform us? We had to insist and wait before we knew which family and clan this child belonged to. We are going to be related to them, though."

"Listen, as for me I think it will be useless, but if you really want it I will not stop you, it is your right to do so."

There was a new silence during which father Sadisa sighed.

"I shall support you in this process. I know that you may have regrets about our sister Kimani's opinion and you would like to reassure yourself by checking that the information given to us is accurate and that our child is not going anywhere, or to anyone. I shall help you. I am going to do better, I shall to take care of this myself."

Father Ebata was reassuring in his remarks to his elder. He had felt his emotion and knew he needed help. He had just lost his wife dramatically and his daughter was going to leave him the next day to live far away from him without knowing when would be the next time he would see her again. His life would change dramatically within a few weeks. He needed a lot of support.

"I will ask a few people I know to check out certain points and I will report back to you regularly. Until I have any evidence to confirm this information I will continue. But having said that, why would anyone want to hide and give false information about his family? Particularly to marry a girl from a family as modest as ours? I would not understand if that turned out to be the case."

"I know," father Sadisa said softly, "but I need to have a clear heart. Thank you for wanting to take care of it."

"It is nothing. It is also a way for me to pay tribute to our late sister. We must always pay tribute to our fallen ones."

Old Yinda arose slowly. He emptied his cup of palm wine and rested it on the shelf in front of him.

"All right, young people, I shall let you continue your endless night. I am going to try to sleep for the short night we have left. You should do the same. Tomorrow is another day."

Father Ebata also stood up.

"I am going to take your advice, senior. I am actually very tired. What a day!! Have a good piece of night, senior Sadisa."

"Same to you. I am going to emulate you soon."

Sadisa remained alone in the concession, among the women of the family who were still doing some domestic tasks here and there. A wedding ceremony took a lot of time to prepare and even while it was happening one had to be vigilant and leave nothing to chance. Thus, some took care of the next day's meals, while others discussed-yet-how all this was going to be presented. Endless talking.

Father Sadisa looked at them with a slight smile. He admired their commitment to the occasion. He then let his gaze wander through the courtyard. He stopped at his wife's grave at the far end. It was discreet, but very present, at the very edge of the barrier. He felt great sadness invading him abruptly. This happened to him every time he looked at it. He thought that today he had to make the effort not to be too dominated by this feeling of distress, but it was rather difficult. But out of love for his daughter, he had managed to stay, at least to appear happy throughout the ceremony. But in the immediate future, he was left alone and his brain began to reseed everything he had repelled during the day.

He got up and walked slowly towards the gate of the yard. He stood at the edge of the entrance. He began to observe the many people still walking outside. There were always groups of artists dancing and singing. There were also stalls of various dishes that still attracted late or particularly hungry candidates. The right word would be rather greedy. He recognized very few faces. Those he recognized were the only ones who were being served with food. At first, he did not pay attention to it. But he eventually found it curious and focused his attention on it to see if he had been imagining things. It was not the case. None of the faces he did not recognize crowded around the food stalls. He observed one, then two, then three stalls. He noticed the same phenomenon. He went out and walked to the end of the alleyway to observe other stalls. He noted that it was the same everywhere. Had the strangers all been fed so much that they were not going to eat anymore? He was tired. He decided not to think about it again and went back to bed. On his way back, he met a few people who thanked him for the beautiful day they had just spent. He told them that they should instead thank his daughter because she was the one who made the choice that had led to the ceremony. These marks of recognition still gave him a little balm in his heart. So he want to bed slightly lightheaded.

6

Day 1

Two days later, with all the arrangements for the departure, the morning passed very quickly. It went all the faster because many had spent much more time than usual sleeping after the second day of the wedding and the short night that had followed. A short new night that had seen the same phenomena repeat themselves. There had still been an incredible number of visitors who came no one knew from where. There had still been food in incredibly abundant quantities and sufficient for all. Once again in the early morning, as a day earlier, all and everything had disappeared, from where they had come without a trace.

By mid-evening, father Sadisa had pointed out to his youngest, father Ebata, what he had noticed the night before between those who fed and those who did not. The latter had retorted that there were so many supply points that it was certainly not possible to really corroborate his claims. Neither of them had formalized it any longer. Father Sadisa had then decided to go to bed. He had got up early because he did not want to miss a single opportunity to watch Nsona before she left. He spent the morning observing her discreetly. He felt an immense pride in the work he had done with his wife to achieve this result of such a young woman.

His job that morning was to oversee her daughter's preparations for her departure. She should not lack anything, either on the way or when she arrived on the spot. She also had to bring presents for her brand new in-laws. Moreover, it was customary for a bride to arrive in her new home with enough to prepare her new husband's first meals, in order to show that she did not arrive destitute at her in-laws. Usually, in addition to all the kitchen utensils given to her by her aunts, the family offered their daughter a goat. But as the journey was much longer than usual, Father Sadisa and the whole family felt that it would be wiser to give her a substantial sum of money that she could use to buy one on the spot. This would avoid the risk of taking an animal that would lose weight during the journey.

Nsona was given loincloths of great value for his future aunts, ceremonial clothes for his future uncles-in-law and some other quality gifts for his future brothers-in-law and sisters-in-law. All this without counting some hard cash for her personal use until she could find an occupation that would allow her not to depend too much on her husband. It was never a good thing to be completely dependent on a husband. Each member of the family had become involved to the point where Nsona realized that she was leaving a family that loved her. Some, she knew, had made sacrifices for her, so that she would be comfortable in her new environment. There was no better proof of love from their side.

The neighborhood was bustling. Nsona was about to move on to her new life. Everyone wanted to see the start of the procession. A procession as had rarely been seen in the hood. It was true that the one who had succeeded in getting her to give up was not just anyone. He was almost as rich as the revered ruler of the empire, some said. He is still much richer, others said. But no one suspected the actual state of the possessions of Tembo, the child of Mbuila, as he had presented himself. If only they had known...

Onlookers crowded in front of the concession of pa Sadisa's house. Little by little, they were asked to step aside as horses were coming. They had been sent by Tembo's family to take care of all the belongings of the young wife. It was an event because few people had the opportunity to see some. Most often donkeys or oxen were the usual transport animals. This time, there were more than half a dozen beautiful nervous and stinging beasts. They were all dark in color. Children looked at them with marveled eyes, filled with a slight fear at the sight of so much power and admiration for those who controlled them. For nothing in the world they would have wanted to miss such a rare show. The mounts were positioned along the family fence. Some well-packed luggage was starting to come out to be loaded. They were all covered with a kind of thick fabric with a pattern that represented ma Kimani's favorite colors and thus made it possible to identify them at first glance. This fabric shone in a beautiful orange yellow adorned with large black and red spots of various shapes. Leather straps firmly hugged each batch. They were hooked on either side of a good half of the horses in perfect balance. Meanwhile, two other mounts were harnessed to solidify them and place a comfortable seat in between them. The last would have been ridden by one of the many companions who accompanied Tembo on his long journeys. He would guide the young woman's horse team.

Very quickly, all the horses were ready to go. There was of course a strong animation in the alley. The crowd kept growing, as if the spectacle offered by the situation was the one that should not be missed. Indeed, all this was remarkable. Just a few moons back, no one thought Nsona would find a party so easily. Finally, she had found an excellent party. Given all that he had been able to implement for his marriage, he was an exceptional party. And what was happening before their eyes only confirmed it. They were not yet at the end of their surprise.

A melody began to rise from pa Sadisa's family court. The women in the family had sung a traditional song which was a series of praises and recommendations for the young woman who was leaving. This song was the first in a series that resonated when the departure was close. The other songs asked the young woman not to forget her own, to be always dignified and to always honor her husband. The crowd outside took the choruses and the verses all together. In the end, everyone started singing without exception. All those who had been jealous of her sang, all those who had slandered the young woman sang, all those who had been turned away sang.

*

"I am happy for you, my daughter. I do not know how to tell you how I feel. I wish you all the best for this new journey that opens up to you."

Pa Sadisa and Nsona had a moment of intimacy which they knew would be very brief. In one of the middle rooms of the family home, they could finally talk quietly after the two frantic days that had just passed.

"Thank you, papa. I am so moved, happy and sad at the same time. I have been in an indescribable emotional confusion for several days."

"It is not surprising, we could be for less! Do you realize what you are going through right now? Would you have imagined it only a few moons ago? I do not think so."

"I do not, either, it is true."

"Well, that is it. All this is only normal. To tell you the truth, I would have been very worried if you had not felt that way. At least it reassures me: you are normal."

She smiled.

"But I would have loved so much mama to also live these moments with us. She would certainly have seen that she was wrong about Tembo's account. He looks so caring."

Pa Sadisa's face darkened imperceptibly.

"Do not worry about it. I am sure that her attitude was dictated by the fear she had of seeing you go. She would have certainly accepted after having seen your happiness. And you are right; I too would have liked her to be with us in these rare moments of happiness."

There was a silence during which he laid a tender look upon her. The chants were suddenly silent outside. It was as if everything had suddenly frozen. One of Nsona's youngest daughters emerges.

"Papa Sadisa, big brother Tembo is coming."

The father and daughter got up. He took her by the arms.

"My daughter, this is the long awaited moment. I recommend you to our ancestors and our almighty god. Let them look after you. I know they never leave us. So we must also think of them in all circumstances. So hand yourself over to them in case of difficulties, you will see that they are still there. Do not forget that when we leave, we do not die, we only go asleep. And someone who sleeps can hear a call. Never forget that. Call upon them and the blessing of our almighty god."

"Thank you, papa. Let them keep you, too. And may God accompany you in all circumstances as he has always done."

*

When she walked out of the house, the bride illuminated by her presence an already sunny day. The many murmurs that still commented on the arrival of her husband gave way to a silence full of admiration.

She was very simply dressed, a simple long orange-red tunic tied at the waist by a linen belt that highlighted her young woman hips. But what impressed most was the hairstyle she sported. It was a clever weaving that mixed her hair with fabric matching her outfit. The whole was unfolded in a fan that adorned her head, reinforced by carved wooden rods. The frizzy hair had been coated with a plant balm that made them brighter than usual, but also had the function of protecting them from possible insects and parasites during the journey. This hairstyle was made to last. What also surprised was the fact that she did not wear it the day before. This meant that it had been achieved during the night. A real feat. Indeed, experts had been taking care of the young woman's appearance for most of the night. There had been six of them working together or taking turns to achieve this result so quickly, which was obviously a real success. Knowing she was observed, she sported a beautiful smile, discovering teeth greatly whitened by years spent rubbing them with the traditional peach root of the region.

The farewell hugs began without her even realizing it. In fact, she did not have time to take the initiative. Her youngest sisters were the first ones to come and hug her. The rest of the family followed little by little, from the youngest to the eldest, from the closest she had seen quite regularly until then to those she saw only occasionally and whom she would therefore see even less. The closer she got to the exit of the court, the more neighbors had managed to break into the protected perimeter that had been improvised by Tembo's escort. Neighbors included friends and childhood friends, friends and friends of her parents, who had all nearly become family members. With them, the effusions were even more intense because they were the people she had been seeing almost every day since she had been a child. Some of them had also played a parenting role as it often happened in a neighborhood with the children who lived there. There was an increasingly uncontrollable hustle around her. The chants had resumed. At first shyly, then much more frankly, they encouraged the girl to arm herself with courage in her new life. They also wished her a good trip to her new home. And finally, they obviously wished her the inevitable fertility in her marriage.

"Greetings to you, Nsona."

Without realizing it, she had arrived in front of her husband, who was waiting for her by the team that had been prepared for her. She looked at him, without giving up her smile. He was impressive in elegance. In front of her, he largely held the comparison. He also wore a light tunic, as the beginning of their journey would be in rather heavy heat. Its color was a dark blue of a very beautiful effect. His head was covered with a kind of feathered toque of a nocturnal bird that Nsona identified as owl feathers. She found it original because the feathers were very beautiful. On the other hand, they were quite light for the occasion.

"Greetings to you, Tembo."

"Did you have a good morning?"

"Yes, thank you. What about yourself?"

He answered with a nod.

"Are you ready to go?" he asked her.

"Yes, let us go."

Before she knew it, he took her with both hands by the hips and hoisted her to the seat on the two horses that had been harnessed for her. She did not find him very athletic, but the way he raised her impressed her. She was not the only one to be. Nsona was not particularly corpulent, but lifting a woman of average size needed to be in a very good shape.

Not far away, Lukuayi was also ready, mounted on her donkey, with the two oxen that bore her effects far fewer of course than those of her friend. As an escort she had her brother-in-law and two of her brothers who were going to spend a few days at her house. They were also riding donkeys.

Tembo walked to his mount, a dark, almost black horse, which carried a varnished wicker saddle and covered with thick white sheepskin. He in turn went to mount his horse after a quick tour of Nsona's family who were present. He waited for the signal from the man who appeared to be in charge of the convoy, cast a final circular glance and then set his horse in motion. The rest of the troop gradually followed. Nsona's team was immediately behind her husband's horse. She greeted her people. Tears flowed gently down her cheeks as she smiled again. Soon, only the kind of tent that covered her seat with thick cushions was visible. Only the many children in the neighborhood who followed the procession loudly could still see her. The songs continued for a long time after the last beast had disappeared.

Pa Sadisa was not outside. He had not attended Nsona's departure. He did not want to have the image of his daughter walking away when he did not know when he would see her again. He preferred to have the smiling, although sad, image he had of her squeezing him against herself. He kept thinking about his wife. He kept thinking about her attitude. He had told his daughter that his mother would certainly have changed her mind about Tembo, but he did not believe a word of it. Ma Kimani had certainly seen something harmful about this boy. The fact that he did not come to say goodbye to him comforted him in this reflection.

But it was a little late to have moods.

*

The procession went gently through Mbanza Miongo, eliciting curiosity, admiration and sometimes envy. It could not help attract attention. In addition to the many horses that carried Nsona's belongings, a dozen others were used to carry Tembo's. It was then necessary to add the half-dozen riders who accompanied them, each on his mount. So there were about twenty horses overall. There were many gestures of encouragement to Nsona because many recognized her. As for those who waved to Tembo, they did so because they recognized the one who seemed to be the master of this impressive procession. Beyond that, they had no reason to do so because they did not know him. No one seemed to know him. This did not prevent him from greeting in turn as if he knew everyone. It made him look really friendly in the eyes of those who saw him for the first time. After all, was there any particular reason to find him unsympathetic?

The jealousy of seeing him next to this beautiful young woman? It would be nothing more than pettiness.

Moments later, they had left the settlement, speeding up the pace to cross the hills that gave its name to it. They were numerous and large. But the route snuck between the flanks, most of which were covered with bushy thickets or undergrowth interspersed with various plantations. The few individuals who worked there greeted the procession which returned their cheers with respect. Notably Lukuayi's companions. They were the most accessible. Their attitude showed that they were indeed children of the land, unlike the men who accompanied the young couple. They also saluted, but did so as coerced and forced to. Moreover, the sun did not seem to succeed them. They sweated heavily and covered themselves more than reasonably since they had left the most populated areas. Was it because they seemed nervous and very agitated? Some came and went, sometimes getting ahead of the group, in the manner of scouts.

"You have nothing to fear around here!" the brothers of Lukuayi had told at them two or three times. "There are no dangerous animals. We could even sleep under the stars without a problem."

But they barely answered them. Continuing to behave like soldiers of a squad on a dangerous mission.

Soon, shortly before sunset, they arrived in sight of Bouaki, the small town that had been Lukuayi's home since her marriage. The group would separate here because there was a fork that would make a detour to the caravan. There was sadness in the eyes of the two young women. They knew they would certainly not see each other for a long time. Going to Mbuila would be quite an expedition for Lukuayi and it would be the same for Nsona if she wanted to come back and recharge with her family.

"My dear, take good care of yourself. Wherever you go, you will learn a new life, get to know new people and adapt. I know you can do it, so I do not worry. But at the same time, life is full of surprises and no one knows what it has in store for us. What may seem like a quiet body of water can hide the worst of surprises. So take good care of yourself, always think of the ancestors, under all circumstances."

"Do not worry, I am in good hands. Who knows? Maybe I shall come back to you sooner than you think? So my friend, my only true friend, pray for me as I will pray for you. The ancestors, by the grace of God, never forget us."

They exchanged one last complicit glance before the beast that bore the young woman was dragged by that of her brother-in-law. In passing, she nodded to Tembo, who answered her back timidly. Each then continued her way, turning her head back from time to time to see the other's procession disappear at the turn of an undergrowth.

*

The hills of Mbanza Miongo had long since disappeared. The landscape had changed and looked more like savannah than forests. It was already dark and the procession was moving quickly to spend the night in the next coming village. It was a place that Nsona already knew for having stayed there once or twice with her mother on a few occasions. So she was still in a familiar territory. During the day, the riders around her had not been very talkative. But as night fell, they seemed to feel more comfortable. Was it the coolness of the night that came to invigorate them? Was it the proximity of a welcoming rest? On his side, Tembo was rather discreet. He would come back from time to time at Nsona to have some news, but nothing more. He was not very talkative either. No more now than during the day. But he seemed more fulfilled.

The path followed by the procession began to be joined by others who arrived diagonally on both sides. Soon other groups joined them. Each time there were the usual courtesy greetings between the different travelers. Conversations were held, acquaintances were made. A woman in the prime of her life, mounted on a donkey, approached Nsona.

"Greetings to you. Where are you going? We are from Kindamba and we are going back to Misonso."

"Greetings to you," Nsona replied. "We left Mbanza Miongo in the middle of the day and we are going to Mbuila."

"To Mbuila? Where is it?" the curious woman asked.

"It is a little after Songo."

"Songo?"

In the darkness of the night that had now completely fallen, she seemed to reflect for a moment.

"No, I do not know such a place. And yet I have already traveled many lands. But I have never been in that one. So what are you going there for?"

"We are going home."

"Oh, that is good. But what did you come so far for?"

The woman felt that Songo and Mbuila were far away because she did not know where it was. With the many trips she had already made, if these lands had been closer, she would have easily identified them. So it aroused his curiosity.

"Actually, I did not come here, but I am leaving here. I am going to join my husband's land. He is from Songo."

"Ah, but that is fine. So you have relatives over there?"

"Relatives? No, I do not."

"Oh! So you have acquaintances there?"

"Uh, no acquaintances either."

The woman appeared to be taken aloe.

"No family or acquaintances? But then, how did you come to know your husband?"

Tembo emerged from the night. He looked briefly but intensely at the woman.

"We will soon be arriving," he said, addressing Nsona.

Then he went back to the front of the convoy not without having cast a last very strong glance at the woman. The latter, feeling a certain hostility in this look which she found indefinable in the darkness, no longer uttered a word and let the group distance itself. Nsona found herself again alone in doing nothing but listening to the sound of the voices of the other processions that the wind would bring back to her.

Further afield the lights of torches finally appeared from the small town that they finally reached: Batika.

*

Batika was one of the last places where one could still say that he was in Mbanza Miongo. Beyond that, really began another land. So this night Nsona was going to sleep one last time in her environment. It was true that she did not yet have the feeling of being away from home. She had not yet had the need to adapt to the people around her. But she did not have to. Their procession impressed by its constitution and its appearance. Moreover, being the wife of the one who was its master, she was immediately regarded by those who knew about it as unapproachable and all were caring for her. So it was her environment that was still adapting to her. What would happen in Mbuila? How would she be welcomed? Would she be accepted?

The convoy had just crossed the most inhabited and lively area. It stopped further in front of a somewhat secluded house. Under the faint glow of the torches, Nsona noticed that it had been built recently. A rather old woman came out.

"Ah, at last!" she exclaimed at their sight.

She approached the young woman, carrying the torch she was holding at face height. She took a long look at her. Surprised by her attitude, Nsona did not react immediately. Then she suddenly remembered what propriety required.

"Greetings to you, mother."

Not knowing her name, she simply called her a mother out of respect for her age. The latter ended up sketching a small smile.

"Greetings, young lady. Why do you not come with me?"

Nsona jumped out of her seat and followed her into the house. Before entering, she glanced interrogatively at Tembo, but Tembo was busy unloading the horses and unpacking the bags with his men.

"Do not worry about that," the woman said. "Let the men do their job. Come and get comfortable."

She pointed to a door at the back of the main room which the front door was facing.

"Behind that door, you will have enough to wash, it will do you great good. There is also plenty to dress you up for now."

The young woman followed the hallway without saying anything and went to wash. She returned a few moments later wearing a white tunic that contrasted with the shadows drawn by the torches that illuminated the room slightly. In one corner of the room, there was a table that she had not noticed when she had entered. A meal that was served. It was hearty and she told herself that it was presented to all, at least not for herself. The woman invited her to sit down to eat.

"I am not going to eat on my own!" Nsona said.

"I am afraid you will," the woman replied." I have already had my meal and as I told you, do not worry about the men. They know what they are doing."

Nsona immediately had less appetite despite the hunger that was pulling her stomach. But she still was going to try to eat the appetizing dishes on the table. There was beef broth, braised fish and warthog stew. All this was accompanied by barely scalded green vegetables, as she loved them. In fact there were only dishes she was fond of. Did anyone know her tastes in the area? It was amazing. A wooden calabash presented her with fresh water, which she served quickly in a cup of the same material. She slowly took a few sips before sitting on the stool that was waiting for her and started to eat.

*

Nsona had finished her meal for quite some time, but she was still alone in the house. A bed had appeared in a corner of the room. That was the word because she had not noticed it until she had finished eating. Perhaps the light from the torches was not intense enough? She waited impatiently for Tembo to come and see her, but he did not. It was the woman, who had come out a few moments earlier, who came back to tell her that he would not come because he had gone to bed.

"But where?" she protested. "I want to go there!"

"Ah? And do you know the place? How are you going to get to where he is? It is not really next door, you know."

Nsona looked at her without saying anything. She thought that this woman was of course complicit in this behavior. But she was silent.

"Anyway, you should not be surprised. Have you ever spent one night with him since you got married? I do not think so. And that will not be the case until you get to Mbuila at home."

Nsona calmed down. That woman was right.

"Who are you to Tembo, mother? Are you a member of his family?"

"How is it he did not tell you whose place you were going to spend the night at? He is very distracted this boy. Anyway, you will ask him. He will talk to you better than I can do."

"But...!"

"Good night. Lock the door behind me."

Saying so, she immediately slipped away, pulling the door behind her.

Nsona found herself alone in the darkness of the room she had just discovered and in which she was about to spend the night. She felt frustrated, uncomfortable and abandoned. How long was she going to have to put up with this? Was that Tembo's usual behavior? She wanted to believe that it was only temporary and that it was certainly due to this new life that he was also going to have to lead. There would be only one moment to endure, the time of the journey. When they reach their destination everything would change and go back to normal, she believed.

She approached the bed and sat there. She thought of hers at Mbanza Miongo. She decided to invoke her ancestors. She prayed for pa Sadisa. She prayed for the rest of the family. She prayed for her friend Lukuayi. She thanked the ancestors and God for the past day and asked them to continue to be by their side for the rest of the journey. Because it would be very long. Then she lay down on the thick cloth that covered the diaper and closed her eyes.

*

Knocks on the door awoke Nsona. She startled in the darkness. The torches had gone out. Was it already daylight? She seemed to have only recently fallen asleep. She sat up on the bed and stretched her ear. Nothing happened. Had she dreamed? She also seemed to have heard voices through the door. She waited again, on the lookout for the slightest sound. But there was nothing but silence. She lay down again and closed her eyes.

7

Day 2

Nsona got up at the first rooster song she heard. She had been awake for a few moments. She had slept deeply despite the nocturnal interlude she had experienced and felt ready to resume the long road that awaited them with her small group. She saw thanks to the dim light that ran through the few cracks through the door and the roof that it was barely daylight. She saw that there was one of her luggage on the other side of the room containing her personal belongings, including clothing. She had not noticed its presence last night. She put this on the account of the fatigue that was hers when she had arrived. So she quickly went to clean up and then dressed in a light tunic like the previous day, anticipating the heat there would be because the season was good for it.

Knocks on the door startled her.

"Young woman!"

She recognized the voice of the woman who had welcomed her. She went to open the door for her.

"Greetings to you. So are you ready to hit the road again? The men have been waiting for you for a while now. It was your husband who wanted us to let you sleep as you wanted."

"But..."

"I know. You will have a snack during the ride, it is planned. You have to take advantage of the cool morning to go fast."

Nsona felt that she had nothing more to say. She went out to see in the nascent day the procession that was already ready to start. She saw Tembo appear in front of her.

"Greetings to you, did you have a good night's sleep?" He asked her.

"Greetings to you. A good night's sleep? Let's say..."

She turned to the woman.

"Did you come knocking on the door last night?"

"Why so? What would I have come to do in the night?"

She then turned to Tembo.

"Someone came knocking on the door last night, I am sure."

Tembo took her by the hips and asked her while hoisting her up to her seat.

"If you are sure, we can only believe you. But when it comes to who it was, we cannot tell. Anyway, we are leaving these places, so let us not think about it anymore."

The procession set in motion in the dim light of the nascent morning. One of the men, whom Nsona did not recognize in the dark, gave her a bag. She opened it for fruit, dried fish and portions of boiled yams that were still hot.

"Thank you," she said.

The man bowed his head back and returned to his occupations. She thought that none of these men ever looked at her in the face. Certainly out of respect given to the man she was the spouse of.

She began to consume her snack. She ate enough to keep up the morning. The further the small group progressed, the more other processions joined them. There would come a time when everyone would go in their direction. But Nsona's convoy was beginning to accelerate and the others, mainly made up of oxen and donkeys, were unable to keep pace. They passed a few processions before finding themselves alone on the way. They soon caught up with another group. But it was leaving the track and heading in another direction. Nsona saw it make a stop, as if waiting for them. But as they passed, no one seemed to pay attention to them. Until Nsona noticed the woman who had spoken to her the day before as they approached Batika. She had her head down, but as the bride passed, she took the trouble to lift her head up and slip her a few words that intrigued Nsona.

"Be careful with yourself, my girl."

Pa Sadisa's daughter had barely understood what she had said that she was already moving away. She had, however, had time to notice the sadness in the woman's eyes. What did that mean? Did she want to send her a particular message? What about? And why? She did not even know her. She thought it was a simple word of kindness from a woman of a certain age to a young woman who could have been her daughter and for whom she had taken sympathy.

She finished one last fruit and began to observe the scenery around her. The environment was clear. There was a tree from time to time, but it was mostly bush that covered the vast plain that stretched on either side of the track that the procession followed. The pace of the horses was high. The journey was long and Tembo had explained that he wanted to go fast to reach their destination of the day at the earliest. Nsona wondered if the animals would last the day. The break they had planned to take in the middle of the day would certainly be very beneficial to them. She noticed that the men accompanying them had split into two groups. One was at the front and the other at the back. So she found herself alone in the middle of the long line with a dozen horses in front and another behind. Usually, an escort would disperse along a convoy. But since the animals were docile and the environment was clear, there was certainly no need to tighten surveillance. However, she felt nervousness on the part of the men. They turned their heads frequently to one side and then to the other, as if they had expected someone or something to arrive. She waited for a moment when Tembo was within earshot.

"What is the matter?" She asked him. "These men look nervous."

He let himself slide to his height.

"Do you think they are nervous? I do not think so. They behave in a very good way. That is all I expect from them. You never know who might happen."

"Who could happen? Since when have our regions been dangerous?"

He dodged the question and looked at her kindly.

"I am really looking forward to coming in and introducing you to all my loved ones."

She smiled at him and looked at him mischievously.

"I am just looking forward to finally being in our own home."

He gave her back her smile and left for the head of the convoy. She followed him with her eyes, thinking of what the woman met the day before had asked her.

"No family or acquaintances in Songo? But then how did you get to know your husband? »

*

By committing to pa Sadisa to learn more about the origins of Tembo's family, pa Ebata knew that he was in charge of a responsibility which he would have to carry out. But that would be a formality. The custodians of collective memory were rather efficient and reliable. In fact, he wondered why pa Sadisa was so keen to have this audit done. Ma Kimani's reaction to refuse her consent for this young man was all the same to a mother who refuses to let her daughter marry someone whose family she does not personally know. And moreover from a faraway land.

But as a responsible man, he had already taken some action to reassure his elder as soon as possible. Thus, the custodian who had provided the most recent information had already been requested. He was initially surprised by such a rather unusual approach to resting questions on a family. But he had bowed to the request, indicating to his sources of information. He explained that the source had taken a long time to pass on the information to him, but that it had still reached him. Finally, deep down, this is what prompted him to take the investigation a little further. Why did the information take so long? Usually they arrived much faster because everything was supposed to be known by one or another member of this corporation and they all made a point of acting as quickly as possible. Pa Ebata had therefore decided to go up the news channel to get a clear heart.

At his request, two emissaries had left for Songo to get as close as possible and thus to have confirmation of Tembo's origins as soon as possible. They had left the day after Nsona had left. They followed the same direction, but much less quickly because they had much more modest mounts. But however, there was no real rush.

*

After a break in the undergrowth at midday, the group had resumed their journey towards Mbuila. The horses had been trotting all morning. Their endurance impressed Nsona. There was something that intrigued the young woman. At that stop, she had noticed that half of the men who were escorting them had faces that were unknown to her. She had asked Tembo why this was so. He had laconically replied that he had men who worked for him in many places and that he was requisitioning them according to his needs. Those who had been replaced would be more useful to him elsewhere than with him.

The landscape had somewhat changed. The terrain was always flat, but the bush had given way to increasingly bushy undergrowth around them. Naturally, the convoy had tightened. They had come across a few travelers who were going in the opposite direction. Each time, the men were nervous, as if they feared something. Nsona still did not understand their attitude. Tembo did not tell her more to help her understand. He was always evasive in his explanations. But she was patient and thought he would finally tell her what he was really getting over. Because she was convinced, something was going on. He was hiding something from her.

A new convoy to cross appeared in the distance. Once more, the men were beginning to show excessive nervousness with respect to the region. Even the horses were nervous and stingy. The convoy was approaching. More than half of the riders went up to the front posts, as if to form a deterrent presence. The convoy was approaching and was now within range of voice. Tembo beckoned his troop to stop. The other convoy kept approaching.

"Who are you?" Tembo's team leader asked.

No answer came back.

"Do you need help?"

Once again, there was no answer.

After a moment during which the two groups observed each other, a man on each side began to get closer to the other. Nsona was watching it all from afar. She saw that there was a conciliabule between the two men. There was obviously a moment of negotiations at the end of which the two men went together towards Tembo. Seconds later, Tembo pointed two horses at his companion. The latter untied them from the rest of the convoy without unloading them and handed them over to the man, who walked away towards his own. From the group came a man who seemed to be the leader. He approached a few steps from Tembo. He wore a large light-colored cape topped with a hood that concealed his face. Then, without saying a word, he turned his heels and dragged his escort into a deafening sound of cavalcade on their mighty horses, lifting a cloud of dust. When it had dissipated, they were gone. The sound of the hooves was no longer even audible.

As if nothing had happened, Tembo beckoned his companions back on the road. Worried, Nsona asked him. He let himself slip again to her. He spoke before she even asked him any questions.

"This was a negotiation that meant not to have us stripped of everything. It also helped protect you."

"But!? Tembo, we are still less than two days away from Mbanza Miongo! This land has always been safe. It is a land where everyone has the opportunity to earn a honest living. It is a rich country with many possibilities for all. Where did these men come from? Why do they need to go after peaceful travelers?

"Times do change, young lady."

He went back to the front posts without worrying any more about her. She remained speechless, her head full of questions. A concern was beginning to rise imperceptibly in it. But she did not realize it yet. The confidence she always had in Tembo had not been undermined. In a way, what was happening had been more or less announced to her. He had told her that the road would be long and fraught with pitfalls. He had also told her that she would in some respects be surprised by certain situations. So she grinned and bore it, and calmed down. The day was still long and it would be useless to tire nervously in these conditions. After all, what had they lost? Just two horses and one load. Their lives were still worth much more than that, no matter what those horses were carrying.

*

The rest of the day went off without a hitch. They soon arrived in sight of their destination of the day. As the day before, other travelers joined them. Greetings were pouring between convoys. Some were obviously used to making the trip and were happy to meet. Negotiations even took place as the convoys advanced. Goods changed ownership. Voices rang out behind Nsona.

"Hey, my brother!" one of the protagonists shouted. "Every opportunity is good for trading! Do not you think?"

"You are right," his interlocutor replied. "But your tools are too expensive, all the same!"

"It is high-quality iron and very strong wood! It never breaks. You can use them for years and years!"

"No, my friend. I have no money to pay you such a price. Go and offer your goods to someone else!"

"It is a shame, my friend. You are losing something."

The track was wide and the man had the opportunity to overtake Nsona's motorcade. This he easily undertook by pushing his donkeys and cart to the max. He came up to the young woman. He looked at her briefly and then continued his run forward. He caught up with Tembo.

"Hey, brother!" he exclaimed." I have enough to allow you to grow tracts of land effortlessly. Very durable iron and wood tools. Akki wood! Are you interested?"

Nsona watched the scene with curiosity. She was impressed by the aplomb with which this man appealed to his potential clients. He really was not cold-eyed. And what an enthusiasm! Certainly it allowed him to do business. She saw Tembo turn his head slightly towards him. Suddenly the enthusiasm faded from the merchant's face. He walked away from Tembo without taking his eyes off him. Then he looked up at her. The young woman thought she saw some concern in his eyes. She also detected some kind of fright. He turned his head and accelerated his pace, as if he wanted to get away as soon as possible and as far away from them as possible. She did not understand. What had happened? Had Tembo said anything unpleasant to him? Why would he do that? He must have felt that Nsona had followed the scene because soon after he came to her.

"You are probably wondering what made this man leave so suddenly."

He had the smile of a child proud to have done something wrong. Before Nsona's interrogative gaze, he continued.

"I told him that a revenant never cultivates."

He scoffed.

"Are you a revenant?" the young woman asked without even a smile.

He seemed surprised. He wondered if she was serious. This time it was Nsona who scoffed.

"You just made the same face as that poor man," she said. "But without the fear. Did you see how you scared him? Please do not do this again."

He nervously steered his horse to the front of the procession as the first houses appeared in the nightfall.

Balanda was a smaller town than Batika. Still, the atmosphere was much the same. But Mbanza Miongo was now far away and the small troop was arriving in the nearby land of Nganga Ngolo. This land was renowned for having healers of a rare skill. Was that justified? In any case, the rumor had been going on for a long time and it was tenacious. This led some charlatans to pretend to be inhabitants of this region. But a charlatan remains a charlatan and sooner or later they were always unmasked.

Just like the day before, they crossed half the houses to arrive on a batisse of carved stones identical in every way to the one in which Nsona had spent the previous night. Intrigued, she looked for her husband. He outstripped her questions.

"I have a few houses like this on the way to Songo. So do not be surprised to see many more in the future."

"I say, you are doing fine. Congratulations! But you could have told me in advance."

"I wanted to let you be surprised by the discovery."

He brought her off her team while some of the men took care of making some effects available to her. Knowing in advance that he would not stay, she walked on her own to the door. A light came from torches that were already lit there. She heard the horses' footsteps quickly move behind her. She had barely stepped through the door that she startled.

"Well, come in! What are you afraid of? You are at home in here."

In front of her, preparing the table for her meal, was the same woman she had left in Batika that morning. She was so surprised that she did not even ask how her presence was possible. Had she not stayed in Batika? But how did she get here before them?

"You know the house, there is everything you need. I have finished what I had to do."

She walked to the door and went out without further formalities.

"Lock well behind me and have a good night's sleep," she said, pulling the door as she disappeared out.

Nsona rushed to lock the door. She felt her heart beat harder and harder. Had she dreamt? There had to be an explanation. Tembo would provide it the next day without a doubt. For now, it was best to calm down. She breathed deeply several times until she felt her heart regain its normal beat. She let her gaze run over the whole room. She saw what she had not seen immediately the night before. A table served and ready, a bed with a thick fabric for better comfort, clothes to wear after grooming and finally her personal belongings to dress in the morning. Maybe she had not been attentive enough the night before. In any case, that night nothing was going to come out of the darkness. It was all there.

She resolved to clean up, thinking that if she started thinking too much about a situation that did not need it, she would start making up stories. Having finished, she went to the table before going to bed after her usual prayer, in which she particularly asked the ancestors to watch over her even more carefully that night.

*

Blows against the door awoke Nsona. Once again, she jump up in the dim light and froze her ears. She also seemed to hear voices behind the door again. The faint glow of the only torch still alive reassured her a little. This time, she decided to get up and get close to the door in a hushed pace. She stuck her ear to it and listened. But no sound resonated. Not even a nocturnal animal noise, nothing. Bold, she wanted to open the door to look outside. She unlocked it and tried to open it. She lifted the big wooden handle that allowed her to maneuver. She pulled the door towards her slowly hoping that it would not squeak. In the silence of the night a squeak would carry away and she wanted to look discreetly outside. Deeming the opening wide enough, she passed her head. She looked to one side and then to the other. She barely distinguished the shape of the nearest houses amidst the few large trees that stood around it. She waited for her gaze to adapt to the darkness. She saw nothing but a dog wandering in the night. She then closed the door to go back to bed.

If she had looked again at that moment, she would have seen a silhouette come off a tree and walk away in the night.

*

"You abandoned my daughter! If anything happens to her, you will forever be responsible for it! I did not want her to marry this man. You knew it! I did not have time to talk to her, but you had time to do it and you did not!"

"But she said herself that she knew this young man and agreed to marry him!"

"And so what?! You should not have given in! What makes you think she told the truth and really knew him?! You should have talked to her! You are responsible! You are responsible! You are responsible!!"

"Talk to her about what?!"

Pa Sadisa awoke with a jolt. What a nightmare! Since his daughter had left, he had felt guilty and what he had just experienced in a dream was certainly not going to calm him down. He stood up and sat down on the edge of the bed. Was he not being too emotional? Did he not let that feeling of guilt control his unconscious? Was it really his late wife, ma Kimani, who had spoken to him in this dream? It was often said that the deceased did not hesitate to come and see their loved ones in their sleep and talk to them. How could he be sure of that? Why not go to a sorcerer to find out more? He shook his head for a brief moment. What was happening to him so that he would come to think of going to see a sorcerer? He thought he was losing his thinking skills. Maybe it was better to go back to bed and let the rest of the night give him advice. He sighed and lay back on the bed.

He thought of his younger brother Ebata. The latter had not yet told him anything about the investigations he said he had been conducting with the guardians of the collective memory. But the deadline was perhaps still a little short to have a significant sequel. He resolved to fall asleep hoping to have a quieter sleep for the remaining night.

If he had known that at the same time, about three days' walk for an ordinary man from Mbanza Miongo, his daughter Nsona had also just woken up with a jolt, perhaps he would not have been so calm.

8

Day 3

Like the previous morning, Tembo was ready very early with the rest of the troop, waiting for Nsona. There were more unknown faces in the group. This time, there were more than half of them. At the beginning of the journey, the young woman asked her husband the question that was tapping her.

"Can you explain to me how is it that the same woman who had received me in Batika was again there yesterday to welcome me while she had stayed there?"

"What makes you think she had stayed in Batika?"

Nsona was surprised by the answer but did not show it. She reasoned loudly.

"So let us consider she also came to Balanda by road. How did she get there before us? I mean, we are moving at an unusually quick pace, because we have travelled almost twice the distance that travelers who would not be equipped with horses like ours could travel. How could she do so? I am asking you."

Tembo leaned on his wife's arguments.

"You said, to go as fast as we do you have to be equipped with horses like ours. If we add the fact that she was not as loaded as we are and that she took a shorter and more suitable route for a single person, then everything explains."

"Was that also part of the surprise of the discovery you reserved for me?"

Tembo put a reassuring look on her.

"I have a feeling that this is what you think, but there is nothing mystical about this woman arriving before us in Balanda."

"I understand, she will still be waiting for me tonight in a house identical in every way to those of the previous two nights, will she not?"

He smiled as he left for the head of the convoy.

"She or another," he said. "Does it really matter as long as you are well received?"

She watched him walk away without answering. After all, maybe he was right. Why was she so intrigued? Had she been treated badly? Did anyone disrespect her? Neither. Although Tembo's attitude might be questionable, she did not really have to complain.

While she had not yet finished taking her morning snack, screams from a crowd further down the side of the track caught her ears. The pace of the convoy slowed down as the few onlookers who clung around an overturned cart began to obstruct the passage. Arriving at the height of the place that attracted everyone's attention, the conversations were more audible to Nsona.

"He leaned under his cart to see what had broken his wheels, but strangely, it collapsed on him!"

"Yes, the poor man had no chance making it. It happened all of a sudden!"

As usual, superstitions entered the dance. They would soon be the explanation over all possible rational explanations for this accident.

"He must have had something to blame himself for such a fate. Who was he? Was he from Balanda or somewhere else?"

"I know him, I had seen him many times before. He came from beyond Mbanza Miongo. He used to come here and sell his tools. He knew it was a very agricultural area."

"In fact, I had heard that he had been having trouble with one of his uncles about the gains due to his sales. Perhaps the dispute had not been resolved. Never have problems with an uncle!"

One of the onlookers laughed.

"Ah, so it was the uncle who had the cart hit him?"

"Certainly! Suppose that uncle died and he still resented him? Well, he was able to take his chance here to get revenge!"

"And you call it a chance?"

"Well... Oh, you understand what I mean, do you not?!"

While passing by, Nsona had time to recognize the man to whom Tembo had made a joke the day before. He was half lying under his cart loaded with tools. This charge rested on his chest and there was a patch of blood that had already been absorbed by the ground. The accident must have happened very early that morning.

"Do not hang around, it is not nice to see."

Tembo had come back to move the procession faster and had spoken to his wife with a hint of guilt in his voice.

"I am sorry I told him what I said to him last night. Who knows what this man's beliefs were."

Nsona nagged him back with a stern air.

"You are not going to imagine that you are responsible for what happened to that man, Tembo? You made a bad joke to him, certainly, but it does not go any further, though!"

He went back forward, leaving Nsona to recover from what she had just seen. Such an end was horrible and was not to be wished on to anyone. What had happened to the poor man? She preferred not to think about it. With no appetite left, she put away what she had left to eat from her morning meal.

*

Once again, the pace of the horses had been very high. They gave the feeling of never weakening. For once, the sun had not been as intense as the previous two days and Nsona felt less tired than usual. So much so that she had taken time to admire the landscape along the way with the chance of seeing some harmless wild beasts. The most dangerous were rarely seen in areas frequented by humans. They had crossed savannahs dotted with bushes and were now approaching a small undergrowth as those had gone through from time to time.

She had had the leisure to rethink about everything that had happened since Tembo and his family had come to her house. Her life had since completely changed. At first, there had been discussions as to whether this request should be acted upon or not. At the head of those, very few, who were opposed to it there had been her mother. She had started convincing one and then the other. Then had happened her sudden death. As a result, everyone had agreed to give her hand to the young man. She herself had claimed to have know the young man and, finally, she agreed to give satisfaction to a suitor after all those she had dismissed. Was it not the most important thing that she herself agreed to this marriage? There was therefore no valid reason to object.

But what no one knew at the time was that she had told a lie. In fact, she had never met Tembo as she had claimed. But she herself would be unable to explain why she had confirmed his sayings. The latter had indeed stated in front of the two families that he knew the young woman, but this was of course not the reality. So why did she not contradict him? Maybe she did not want to embarrass him? A shame that would then have certainly affected the young man's family. This would have been even more serious and might have resulted in resentment towards her even though she would not have been responsible. But she had found him a friendly and handsome boy, although particularly young unlike many others who wanted to marry her. So she claimed to know him, committing the irreversible. How could she then have reversed her statements without covering herself with ridicule? Instead, she imagined her father telling her, "You cannot fill a gourd with the water that has spilled on the floor". So she had to assume the situation.

She then remembered her conversation by the water side with her friend Lukuayi. The words she herself had said and which had come true. She did not even realize it. She had pointed it out to her shortly after her marriage: she had married the first who had come for her. If, as her friend had warned, a bad spirit had heard her, did that mean that Tembo was one? Nonsense! Now she too was delirious, like all those people who believed in the existence of the occult forces that could act among the living. She was not one of them and she was not going to start giving credit now. Tembo had simply arrived at the right time and he had the merit of pleasing her. That is all there was to it. The rest was just imagination.

The procession stopped abruptly. She raised her head and tried to see what was causing it. Further ahead of the first horses, she distinguished a silhouette arched in the middle of the track, in the shade of the trees. She had trouble distinguishing a face, nor could she say whether it was a man or a woman. On the other hand, she could think that it was not a rich person if she considered her clothing, which was made of old patched fabrics. Nsona, however, did not understand why the procession had to stop.

"Tembo, what is going on? Is a single person on the track enough to stop our progress?"

There was no answer. She saw her husband cautiously heading towards the figure. The latter stood up. She was finally able to distinguish the worn face of an old woman. A very old woman, about whom she wondered what she was doing there, all alone, in the middle of an area so deserted by all inhabitants and above all so wild. Just as on the previous day with the group of riders who had faced them, there was a discussion between Tembo and the old woman. It seemed to Nsona that it lasted an eternity. She saw the old woman raise her arms several times to the sky, as if she were disputing the words of her interlocutor. Yet there was no audible burst of voice. The contrast was surprising.

There were still a few long moments after which Tembo beckoned to one of his men. The latter came up to his height. He said a few words to him. The man returned to the convoy. Nsona remembered the scene the day before when she saw him detach two new horses and hand them over to the old woman. The latter received them firmly. To her surprise, Nsona saw her ride one of the horses, address her husband one last time and then walk away. But she did not walk away on the track, either in a way nor the other. She steered her mount out of the way and slowly plunged into the thicket and trees that surrounded them. Soon after she could no longer be seen.

Tembo nervously signaled to his men to resume their march. Knowing that she was certainly asking questions, he came back to her. He sported a broad smile, as if he were satisfied with himself.

"Do not worry," he told her. "We have not lost much. But for this old lady, I think it is a great service that we have done to her."

"That is, what?"

"Well, she convinced me to help her and her family. They are really in need. She has an injured son who can no longer support her family. He cannot even move."

"She convinced you, you say? Yet I had the feeling that she was preaching to you, even more, she was threatening you. Am I deluding myself?"

"She was a bit vindictive, that is true. But that was a bit normal given what she explained to me. She is on the edge, which is obvious. Do not worry, everything is fine."

He turned his heels and went up to the front of the procession. They had considerably accelerated their pace, as if everyone wanted to get out of this place as quickly as possible. In fact, Nsona quickly realized that the horses were galloping. They were galloping at a speed she did not imagine was possible given the loads they were carrying, not to mention her own hitch. And yet she did not seem to feel it shaking so much. On the contrary, it moved in a comfort that was more than acceptable. They left the undergrowth and found themselves in an area of endless bushes. A kind of landscape that Nsona discovered for the very first time. The bushes were green, but sparse on an arid land that contrasted with the one they had just left. They had not met anyone since they had met the old woman. Nsona looked beyond to her husband who led his troupe with enthusiasm and conviction. She thought it would be nice if he were in such good shape when they would arrive in Mbuila.

*

"What have you learnt? What am I going to say to my eldest?"

Pa Ebata was visited by one of the men he had instructed to inquire with the guardians of the collective memory. They were not relatives, but had been recommended to him by a close friend who held them in high esteem for their abilities of seriousness and rigor. It had been three days since he had asked them to proceed as quickly as possible in order to reassure Pa Sadisa. The man himself had asked to meet him as soon as possible. Was there a problem?

"Forgive me, but before I answer your question, I shall first ask you another one. This young man who married your child, did you know him before he showed up at your house?"

Pa Ebata was surprised by the question.

"No, only the girl knew him."

"Did you know even one member of his family?"

"I cannot answer you positively either, because we did not meet them until the evening of their visit."

The man expressed surprise at the news that a family had come forward at nightfall to propose. Pa Ebata had pointed out the exceptional nature of their acceptance, but the man could not believe the lightness they had shown. They should not have received this family, but should have postponed the meeting until at least the next day. And why not two days later, while taking time to find out?"

But these remarks were beginning to intrigue pa Ebata.

"You worry me with your remarks. I am starting to think we have done something stupid in accepting this union."

The man did not answer instantly. He took the time to reflect before speaking.

"One thing that is certain is that there is no very clear answer so far when I ask questions about this young man and his family."

Pa Ebata protested slightly.

"There is nothing new in what you are telling me. That was the case when we first took the information some time ago."

"Yes, that is exactly what I am talking about. This information should therefore be known to people who gave it recently. It is not that far in time! But instead, it is as if the subject is new to them. They seem to have forgotten everything."

"You are right, it is amazing. What does that mean?"

"I am afraid it is going even further. I mean, it seems to me that no one really wants to talk about it. As if it were... Embarrassing."

Pa Ebata reflected for a moment.

"Embarrassing? When you are embarrassed it means that you blame yourself for something. Could they have lied? But why?"

"I am not saying so. In any case not yet, but the attitude of the interlocutors I have had so far seems surprising to me. But it is something else that worries me. I have not heard from my colleague since the last two days. Usually he gives me news every night at least by someone of his progress, but this time I still have nothing. This is not normal."

"Where did he go?" Pa Ebata asked.

"Not far from here, just two days' walk away, to Mpangala. It is the guardians' major place. They all meet once a season to take stock of their knowledge. So I think he will find definitive facts about the information you want to know."

"Oh, he is certainly just late. He will certainly soon give a sign."

The man was silent for a moment. He took a deep breath.

"I hope you are right. You know, I have seen some amazing things in my life."

*

When they arrived in Nzila Kumi, the procession had been galloping non-stop since the sun had begun to drop in intensity. Sunsets were rather slow in the area, which had allowed them to go beyond the stage planned that day. Nsona had protested to stick to their plan, but Tembo had decided that they should try to save time on their forecasts. So they had gone by in a gale through Bopema. She had hardly had time to see a population stunned to see horses passing by that exuded such impressive power. Horses that sapped, blew and also emanated a nervousness that made them unapproachable. But this pace had, of course, largely dropped as Nzila Kumi approached. Once again, Nsona and her group found themselves among other travelers arriving in this community. There were more people than usual for the simple reason that Nzila Kumi was a traffic hub that connected several lands. Visitors came from everywhere, from all directions.

Once again, they crossed the whole town before arriving at a new house similar to the previous two. But this time, the door was closed. Tembo himself walked to the small building and pushed the door. He beckoned his men to unload the necessities and to take care of preparing the premises. They executed and everything was ready very quickly. Soon after, Nsona was alone again at her table after grooming.

But she did not have much appetite. She was thinking about her own. To all those she had left at home in Mbanza Miongo. So what had happened to her to let herself be drawn in this way? She had certainly wanted to find someone to start a home, but she had not imagined that this would happen. She had never thought that a stranger would ever show up and that she would accept his request so easily. And above all, that her people would let her go just as easily. Her father, who was usually so careful and demanding about the origins of the suitors, had for once contented himself with the meager information that had been provided by the guardians of the collective memory. It was true that the circumstances were rather peculiar with the atmosphere that had been around her successive refusals and also the death of her mother. Tembo had simply benefited. Or did he take advantage of it? Did he feel or know that the situation was such that he would have a great chance of being given her hand? But coming from so far away how could he have been so well informed about such a situation?

She finished her meal and prepared to spend another lonely night. She drew closer to the goods that the men who escorted them had made available to her as they did every night. There were several of her clothes and she had a choice of what she could wear the next day. Definitely a delicacy from Tembo. He could have provided her with only the bare necessities, but he did better in order to put her at ease. She sat down on the bed, casting one last circular glance before closing her eyes and making her last prayer of the day.

*

The knocks were a little lighter this time than the previous nights, but strong enough to wake her up again. She sat up on the bed. Her heart was beating strongly. She heard sort of voices that seemed to sound just behind the door. Shards of voices that looked like a rather violent quarrel. She listened to try to understand what they were saying. But all became suddenly quiet. As if those she had heard or thought she heard knew that she was trying to listen to them. She got up and walked slowly, as silently as possible towards the door. Mastering her fright, she unlocked it and tried to open it. The door resisted. She tried again by ensuring a better grip, without further results. She resumed with both hands and drew with all her might, to no avail. It was just blocked. She withdrew back slowly, surprised and disconcerted. She looked around and noted an element that had never caught her attention: there was no other opening than this one door.

She went to the back of the house where the small toilet room was located. It seemed to her she had seen an opening. There was one, but it was only used to remove moisture that could accumulate there. Under no circumstances could it be used to extract oneself from the premises. She then returned to the main room. There, she also saw openings, but simply ventilation chimneys that pierced the terracotta and stone ceiling of the small building. What could she do? Try to break down the door? What strength and what did she have at her disposal to do so? And what would she find out there? Who would she find outside? What if the noise she had heard had nothing to do with her? Why not wait wisely for the day to rise and Tembo to pick her up, as usual? He left her every time with such casualness and confidence that he seemed to think that nothing could happen to his wife. So why would she not trust him? She resolved to lie down again. She waited for fatigue to come and close her eyes again.

9

Day 4

That morning, Lukuayi was quietly returning from the small market in Bouaki when she met one of the women who were present alongside Tembo at his wedding to Nsona in Mbanza Miongo. She approached her.

"Good morning, mother. How are you?

The woman smiles at her.

"Good morning, young lady. I am fine thank you. And how are you?"

"I am fine too, thank you. Do you remember me? I am a friend of Nsona, Tembo's wife."

"…"

"Please, Nsona and Tembo! The beautiful wedding that took place a few days ago in Mbanza Miongo! At least if you do not remember me, you cannot have forgotten such an event, can you?!"

"Well, forgive me, but I have no idea of who or what you are talking about. What are these spouses called?"

Lukuayi seemed surprised, but she still answered the question.

"Nsona. Her husband's name is Tembo and he is from Songo."

She looked at the woman. She recognized her without hesitation. She had been among those who had attended Tembo at the wedding. She was even one of the most active in the delegation. She had given the impression of being an important member of the family.

"Songo ?... Tembo ?... Nsona ?...."

The woman pondered for a while. She gave the sensation of making the effort to rummage through her memory.

"Forgive me, young lady, but I really do not know who you are talking about."

Without wasting any more time, she turned her heels and left before Lukuayi could react. As she disappeared among passers-by, the young woman decided to run after her to clear up this situation, which was beginning to weigh on her nerves. She rushed, shoving a few people in the process. But the woman was no longer visible anywhere. She asked a few people after her, who did not understand who she was referring to.

"A woman of a certain age, with a red and orange headdress on her head!"

"You would not have seen a spirit?" A man teased her. "You know there are a lot of them on market days!"

Laughter erupted around her. She glanced one last time around her, but without success. It was quite amazing. Not only had this woman stated that she did not know that a wedding ceremony had taken place a few days ago, but she had also stated that she did not know the bride and groom, including the groom of whom she was one of the most present members of the family. Lukuayi was certain of that. What should she think of such a situation? Who could she talk to about it? She was not a person who would leave a question unanswered. She recalled that the family had given an address to a dwelling where it was possible to see Tembo when he came to Mbanza Miongo. Other of his relatives, close or not, lived there permanently. She would go there and get this matter clear. This would allow her to reassure herself about her friend's choice.

What was becoming of her friend ? She thought of Nsona, wondering how her trip was going on and whether she was happy with her choice. After her few days of walking she should now be a long way off. She had no idea how far away her friend was. She decided that as soon as she would arrive home, she would set out again for Mbanza Miongo to unravel the mystery of the woman who had forgotten a member of her own family.

*

This time, not only had all the men who accompanied them changed, but they were even fewer than the day before. Nsona also noticed that the number of horses had decreased. Among the twenty animals at the beginning of the trip from Mbanza Miongo, there were only half of them this morning, including his own. What had happened that night? She had barely had the opportunity to talk to Tembo since they has resumed their journey. He was very busy directing his men and giving them instructions. He had not done so much before. He seemed worried. It was as if he expected to meet hostile people. Was the region that uncertain as to cause so much worry? Or was there a connection to the bursts of voice she had heard in the night? If that was the case, who had to do with her husband and why?

For once, the sky was cloudy. Many black clouds accompanied them since they had left Nzila Kumi, the locality of the ten roads. It had been called so for many years, because of the ten roads that linked many regions to it. Yet on that day there was an eleventh path that the group went through. If Nsona had known that there were usually only ten lanes that joined at this crossroads, she would certainly have wondered.

But she did not know that. Unable to talk to anyone every time she arrived in a locality, she could not gather even a small piece of information. She would probably not have followed Tembo so easily.

More than half of the morning had passed and the horses had once again started galloping frantically as usual. But it seemed to the young woman that this time they were even faster than ever. The pace was such that Nsona could not speak to her husband, or even call him. She would have to wait until the following break. She would still have time to ask herself a whole set of questions that were tapping her mind.

Finally the pace of her mounts began to slow down and that of the others with. They were approaching a large forest whose appearance, combined with the dark clouds that still threatened in the sky, did not augur anything welcoming. The small troop stopped a few hundred steps from the trees to rest and let the horses recover. Slowly, with an unusual silence and a slowness that contrasted with the speed that had carried the horses to this stop, the men began to unpack some goods to extract the meal for the occasion. They set up as usual a place to sit for both spouses. So they soon sat down. A moment that Nsona had been looking forward to since the beginning of the morning. But the first question she asked had nothing to do with what she had on her heart since the morning.

"What is going on?" she asked.

Tembo looked surprised.

"What do you mean by that?"

She pointed the men with her chin while she was putting a piece of dried fish in her mouth. He pretended to still not understand.

"I can see that they have an unusual attitude. So what is going on?"

Nsona had noticed that none of the men had spoken to Tembo since the morning and that they even had trouble talking to each other. There was a tension and it was palpable. In fact, there were two distinct groups that looked at each other almost with suspicion. Neither seemed to want to eat. They seemed to be watching at each other's horses.

Tembo was still not answering. She showed a hint of irritation in her voice.

"Would you answer me? What is going on?"

He looked at her calmly.

"There was just a clash between two of them last night. I have tried to reason them, but it is not obvious when there are two people who do not want to be reasoned. Now there are two groups that are almost opposed. We shall have to deal with it, but I think it is going to fade away with a little time.

She took advantage of the attention he gave her to ask him the question that was burning her lips.

"Is it to you that I owe having been locked up last night?"

Nsona knew that Tembo had been present that night outside the house where she had slept. One of the voices involved in the outbursts she had heard was his.

"Yes, it is me. You are a long way from home and nights can be scary in an unknown place. You may then be tempted to commit a reckless act, such as opening your door in the middle of the night and risking coming face to face with a stranger or whatever. That is what you did two nights ago and I did not want it to happen again."

He had finished his words looking her straight in the eyes. She held his gaze for a moment. It was the first time she had done it for so long. She was impressed by the deep and intense look of such a young face. She seemed to discover the young man. In a flash, she recalled her thoughtless words with her best friend, the terms of her hand's request and then her surprising acceptance. The woman who had advised her to pay attention to herself a few days earlier came back to her mind, as well as the eyes of the tool seller before the scene of his death on the side of the track. She recalled those nights when she woke up after hearing bangs on her door. So many situations lived in such a short time! She thought there was something unusual going on. What if popular beliefs were not just beliefs? What if a bad genius or a bad spirit, no matter which, had really seized her words that night at the water edge with Lukuayi?

"Are you the one who came knocking on my door in the middle of the night?"

"Why would I do that?" the young man exclaimed.

She did not answer and continued to eat. He had come to make sure that she could not go out in the middle of the night. But what or who did he want to protect her from? Was there a threat to her? And why?

"What do you want to protect me from? What is so dangerous or who is going to hurt me so badly that I should not go out at night?"

"I am just planning. I am not going to wait until something happens to find out if there is a danger, should I?"

His argument may have been admissible, but curiously Nsona was not convinced. Again, she did not answer. A burst of voice suddenly resonated.

"My expectations are not met, Tembo! So I am going back into the world! I have nothing more to do here!!"

After saying so, the man got up. He approached the beasts and untied two of them, laden with goods. Two of the other men tried to intervene.

"You do not have the right!" one of them said. "It is not in the practices! You still have to wait to be sure!"

But they were prevented by others while the rest watched the scene without any visible emotion.

"No," one of them said, "he can do whatever he wants. We are not far away and he may decide to withdraw!"

Oddly enough, despite the palpable tension, everything went without any violence. The man grabbed the two horses and walked away after waving to one of the men who was watching the scene to join him. They thus moved away, in the opposite direction to that followed by the group before this surprising break, as if they were returning to Nzila Kumi.

Tembo stood up and watched the scene without reacting. Of course, this surprised his young wife.

"But! You just let him go so with your belongings?! What does that mean? What is going on here?!"

"Calm down. It is not my property anyway. Besides, the only good that I really have here, and by far the most precious, is you. And as long as they do not go for you..."

"Should there be a reason to go for me?" she asked him.

He looked at her, but did not answer. Then he went to the men who had stayed.

"It is time to go on!"

He then turned to the young woman.

"The most important thing is what you yourself think: would they have a reason to go for you?"

Nsona felt destabilized. But once again she did not answer. She also stood up and let herself be installed on her team. The rest of the convoy then set off and began to sink between the trees, which revealed a path that did not seem to have been widely used, while in the distance thunder rumbled.

*

Lukuayi arrived late in the morning at Mbanza Miongo. The first thing she did was to go to pa Sadisa to greet him. She could not have been there so close to him without going to see him. Her best friend's father was also hers. The latter was very happy to see her again so soon.

"What brings you back to us so quickly, my child?"

She did not want to worry him. He must have been pretty upset after everything that had changed his life lately.

"I came here to settle some small matter and take the opportunity to do some shopping. Here, I brought you some of the salt that my husband sells."

She handed him a raffia bag that weighed much heavier than a little salt. A big smile lit up his face.

"Oh,… Ah! How good it is! I have very little left too. With what has happened recently there has been a much higher than normal consumption. Thank you and thank you to your husband. I know he is behind this."

She could not restrain a little laugh.

"We cannot hide anything from you, pa Sadisa. You always guess what is going on!"

A silence was set up for a brief moment, which the young woman broke.

"How are you, papa?"

He took a deep breath before answering.

"It is difficult, my child. It is difficult, but what can we do, so is life. People are born, die, come, and leave. There is always movement around us. We must adapt to the desires of our ancestors through the grace of almighty God. He is the one with the whole decisions. So I adapt."

She took his hands and squeezed them slightly.

"You are not alone, papa. I know it is difficult, with the passing of mama and the departure of my sister Nsona. For me too it is difficult. Differently, but it is also difficult. I shall not leave you on your own. Do you hear me? I shall always be by your side. I am your daughter now, while waiting for Nsona to come back to see us. I do not know when, but she will be back. That is for sure. It cannot be any other way."

He gave her back her embrace.

"May God hear you, my child. And above all, bless you. You are so adorable."

"You deserve it. You have always been there for us throughout all our childhood. It is now up to us to give you back what you have given us the whole time we have been growing up."

The old man sighed. His eyes lit up.

"It is a pleasure to see such recognition. I congratulate you, my child."

They hugged their hands one last time and the young woman took leave. She took a quick tour of her childhood neighborhood, greeting everyone before heading for the address indicated by Tembo's relatives.

Beneath her large dress in cheerful colors, the beginning of the roundness of her belly was not so noticeable. No one could have suspected that she was pregnant, much less with what she was undertaking; an action requiring energy, as usual. On the way, she met a few more people who recognized her. In particular, she met an old man who once lived in the same alley as her family, but had moved not far from the area where she was going.

"So how is your dear husband?" He asked her.

She answered him with a broad, wistful smile. Another souvenir of her childhood came back to her mind. She briefly remembered herself with Nsona, running into the man's yard many years before with her daughter, who had suddenly died when they were barely teenagers.

"He is fine, thank you."

"And what is it that brings you around? You are not really home in these places, are you?"

"Yes, I know. I am going to visit Nsona's in-laws."

"Oh yes!" he said in a suddenly very enthusiastic voice. "It is true that Nsona got married, too. I had heard about this marriage, but unfortunately I had not been able to attend. On the other hand, her in-laws are well known now, after such a marriage. I did hear it was a great ceremony?"

"Yes," the young woman replied, laughing. "To a point you cannot even imagine!"

"Good, so much the better," the man said, smiling.

Then his mine scowled a little.

"So you are going to see her in-laws. That is nice of you. That is very good. But they cannot be seen often around. And when they are, it is almost never the same ones you see. You would think that they come and go and that their home is only a crossing point. It does not seem to be a permanent resident in this beautiful house. It is so impressive that few visitors enter. There are silly rumors about those who came out of it. Always the same when you want to slander successful people. In any case, it appears that the house would not be frequented. But it is as always nonsense."

He was silent for a moment and looked at the young woman.

"Did you tell anyone you were going to see your friend's in-laws?"

Lukuayi seemed surprised by the question.

"Uh, not really. Why are you asking?"

"For nothing. But it is always better to tell your people where you are going. Take care of yourself, my child and see you next time."

They greeted each other and left after pointing out to the young woman in which direction and where to go to reach her destination. She was still intrigued by the old man's words, even though he had afterwards tried to reassure her. A house that was not to be frequented was a dwelling deemed to have some connection with dark forces. But as he had said, it was common to assert such statements to denigrate those who had succeeded by implying that they had made a deal with evil spirits and thus excuse their own failures. So she went on her way without paying any more attention to his words.

Soon after, she arrived in view of the famous house. It was indeed impressive. It was of a height equivalent to at least three men. Its façade carved from huge stone blocks was of an indescribable beauty. She looked around. There were a few other houses, but not in any way related to this one. In fact, all the others were quite away and seemed to give to it room to be even more visible. It was surrounded by a brown varnished wooden fence that rose until her shoulders. So she could see inside before she could access it. High grass bordered the fence, giving an impression of abandonment. She walked along the wide planks that separated her from the entrance, looking inside without distinguishing anyone. She

201

arrived at the entrance. It consisted of two large black tree trunks placed on each side and which reached well above her head. They were connected by a kind of equally black wooden arch covered with white flowers to which she did not pay attention. This did not prevent her from continuing. She pushed the fence easily, and came in wondering since when the construction had been there.

"It has been here forever!"

She startled. In front of her, on the left of the driveway leading to the entrance to the house, stood a young man who had just answered the question she had not asked. There he was, standing and looking at her calmly, with no emotion in his eyes.

"Pardon me…?!" she reacted in a reflex of surprise.

"Oh, will you leave her alone! She did not ask you for anything. Always there to brag about this house. Disappear!"

Lukuayi turned her head to the right of the aisle to see a very old woman sitting on a wicker stool looking at her strangely.

"Hello my child, do approach. Who are you? It is nice of you to visit us like this. Very few people come to visit us. You cannot imagine the joy it gives me."

"Good morning, mama. I am a friend of Nsona, Tembo's wife. I came to Mbanza Miongo and I thought it would be nice to come and see you."

The old woman looked down at the ground, dubious.

"Nsona? Tembo? Oh, I am so old, I do not even remember who you are talking about. And then, you know, so many of us live here."

At that moment, Lukuayi heard a noise coming from the house.

"Oh yes," the old woman said, pointing her finger at the door, "she must know what you are talking about."

"Thank you."

The young woman turned to go to the house, casting one last glance at the young man. But he was gone. She had not even heard him leave. He had disappeared just as the old lady had asked him to. She moved towards the house. Arriving on the threshold, she glanced one last time at the old woman. But she had also disappeared. How strange was this court where people appeared and disappeared...

Still, she went up the steps that separated her from the door and advanced slowly towards it. It was wide open and it was very dark. Something bothered her about this so large construction, but she could not identify what it was.

"Hello!! Is there anyone in?"

Faced with the silence that answered her, she pretended to return.

"Do not go, Lukuayi."

The young woman stopped and turned to the door. She suddenly felt uncomfortable. What did she after all come to do here? Simply because a woman had not remembered the marriage, she had decided to make the trip from her home to here. What if she was the one who got the wrong person? What if she was the one who confused this woman with the woman she thought she had seen at the wedding?

"Come on, come on," the woman said softly. "Please come in."

She had recognized the voice she had heard that morning in Bouaki. In the darkness of the room, she recognized the woman she had met when she returned from the market. Suddenly a torch lit up behind her and Lukuayi saw another figure inside the room. In fact, it was a corridor leading to an area that was not lit by the torch that had just illuminated the entrance. She hesitated. A loud inner voice told her that she should not cross the threshold of this house. She thought that having already entered the court was certainly not a good decision after having seen these two people whom she had not seen from the outside. She still did not explain their appearance. Neither did she their disappearance.

"Uh, forgive me, mama, but I would rather stay outside. I find it hard to see in the dark when it is daylight."

The woman hesitated. She glanced briefly at the figure behind her and finally came out. She was dressed differently from the morning, but she was she one she had met in Bouaki. Lukuayi was convinced of this. She continued to follow her instincts and decided to pretend that nothing had happened earlier in the day.

"Do you know my name?" she asked the woman.

"Of course," she replied." How could I have forgotten Nsona's best friend after you had a presence at that lavish wedding?"

"Oh yes?" the young woman said with a small smile. "On the other hand, I beg you to forgive me but on my side I have not been able to hold yours."

"It does not matter, there were so many people. It is no wonder you do not remember everyone's names. There were far too many people and often not always the ones they were before."

She asked the figure to bring them stools. He was a middle-aged man that Lukuayi did not recognize. He laid the objects and returned to the darkness of the hallway after looking emotionlessly at her. This woman was the only one Lukuayi could identify as having been present at Nsona's wedding. If the others were also members of Tembo's family, then she did not remember meeting them at the various ceremonies. The young woman wondered what the woman had meant with her last sentence. She did not dare to ask. All she thought about now was leaving.

"You have a very big house," she said.

"Yes, Tembo comes from a family that has great means. I can even say very great means."

There was a silence.

"If my estimates are good," the woman said, "Tembo and Nsona should not be far from their destination."

"After only four days?" Lukuayi exclaimed. "I thought it would take twice as long as that?"

"You are talking about ordinary travelers. But with the beasts they have, they will undoubtedly have moved much faster than usual. In fact, they are not ordinary travelers."

"Ah!" Lukuayi said.

She was beginning to think that there was much more to say about Tembo and his family than Nsona's family knew. The woman's words were very enigmatic. And besides, why had she not said her name yet? She would not insist.

"Any way," the woman said, "I know that his parents will finally be happy to see him bring Nsona back. They have been waiting for this for a long time."

"How long has it been? Tembo is still very young, do you not think?

"Youth is relative, my child. One can be considered young in one land and not as young in another. It is just an appearance, believe me. It all depends on the experience you have.

Lukuayi was intrigued.

"Does Tembo have such a great experience of life? Then he would be a lot more mature than he looks."

"Is not the decision he made to go to Nsona's parents and get married a sign of maturity?"

They spoke for a while more about things and others before Lukuayi decided to depart.

"Are you leaving, already? I did not even think about offering you a drink!"

"No, thank you. Never mind, I am not thirsty anyway."

She stood up.

"So good day and see you soon."

She had no intention of shaking the woman's hands. She wanted to avoid such a gesture at all costs. Her instinct advised her. There are popular beliefs that go through generations, which are considered to be nonsense. Some may seem far-fetched as long as you just hear about them and if they are isolated. But when several of them are telescoped, then it is normal to ask questions and start to doubt. She thought of everything that had happened and that she had observed since the morning. Several beliefs had manifested themselves in a single day. If this woman was indeed the one she had started to imagine that she was... But that could not be possible. She was certainly delirious. Moreover, it would not be polite to leave without shaking the hands of this woman who had just received her, even if she found this situation strange. In spite of herself, she made the mistake she wanted to avoid at all costs. A mistake in any case if one stuck to popular beliefs.

She bent down and took respectfully the woman's two hands into hers. She shook them respectfully as she returned her embrace with a mischievous, cold look that sent a shiver into the young woman's back. They let go of their hands without exchanging a word and Lukuayi walked out of the yard. Once outside, she glanced one last time behind the fence. The woman was missing, as were the stools. Had she already gone back into the home so fast? She looked around. There was no one near the fence. She even noticed that the few individuals who passed seemed to do so as far as possible from the construction. She had not noticed this when she had arrived. Some were sneaking their eyes at her. She then recalled the words of the old man she had met before arriving.

Popular beliefs have no basis, but do they not always have a background of truth or at least an explanation that justified them? Most of the time, it was someone who had heard someone else who had said that such a person had experienced such a situation out of the ordinary. Nothing could ever be proven and yet the belief was tenacious and often paralyzed mentalities. Only those who suffered them could testify, when they still could. However, they were hardly given credit. But most often they could not because for them it was too late. So only speculation went on well. The person would have encountered a bad spirit and his gaze would have been caught. This meant his life had been captured. The person would have been grazed or touched by an evil spirit. He would also have just spoken with it and his breath would have been contaminated. This would condemn the poor individual. And if one had the misfortune to enter a house or place frequented by evil spirits then one really had no chance of staying alive. But there was no evidence. No one had ever been able to establish a cause-and-effect relationship proving all of these allegations.

As she threw her last glance at the house, she understood what had bothered her from the beginning without figuring out what it was. The huge building had no other opening than the front door. There was not even aeration on the terracotta roof. There was just that one and only front door.

*

The group was moving in the rain, a pouring rain. In her hitch seat, Nsona, protected by a waxed-skin cloth treated with vegetable fat, was dry. The pace of progress had, of course, dropped considerably because visibility was very low. But they were still moving rather fast. The entire luggage had been protected by a canvas like the one covering the young woman. All the men had also donned a dark waterproof cape that wore a hood and covered their heads. They were impressive, even intimidating in the dimness of the trees, accentuated by this very unfriendly weather. Yet

Nsona felt comfortable. This rain had brought freshness. This changed from the usual heat of the season. Since their mid-day break, Nsona and Tembo had not had the opportunity to talk to each other. She wondered about what he had said to her, but could not find an answer. Only he could give it to her, but she did not think he would give it to her. He was always enigmatic, evasive. That was beginning to worry her.

While she was still in her reflections, a rumble rang out behind the small troop. Half the men turned to the newcomers to face them. Surprisingly, their attitude was that of people who seemed to expect this situation. They lined up tightly in front of the arriving cohort. It was upon them in a few moments. Fifteen men, all with hooded capes, in all respects identical to those carried by Tembo's group, including himself if not for the white color. They also moved into tight rows before one of them, apparently their leader, detached himself and advanced towards Tembo's companions.

"Who are you? We are not aware of your passage through this forest!"

He was aggressive in his expression. A kind of aggressiveness that portended a penalty if you did not have an explanation that would suit him. His voice was deep and low. It easily dominated the pounding of large raindrops on trees and on the ground. His face was barely visible to Nsona. Having trouble looking behind her from her seat, which made her rather static, she could hardly see his face. While she was still making a great effort to try in vain to see what was going on behind her, she saw Tembo pass by her to go to the man who had just spoken. He was moving his mount forward slowly but determinedly. His face was expressionless, as if nothing was happening.

"These places are not open to all. So I repeat, who are you?"

Tembo's companions strayed to let him pass and face the man. No sooner had he passed them than he dropped his hood halfway, discovering his face sufficiently for the man to see him.

"Oh, that is you?" he said.

He had lost all the aggressiveness he had had so far in his voice.

"So that is fine."

He turned around to join his men. As his men began their cavalcade, he turned one last time to Tembo.

"Remember, you do not have much time left!"

He then followed his men, sneering. They disappeared into the darkness of the forest in a cloud of rain vapor and wet sand lifted by the horses that had started to gallop at an even more impressive speed than those at which those of Tembo moved. These animals were so similar that they would have been thought to have come from the same breeding. Soon, the pounding of raindrops all around them was the only noise the band could still hear.

Tembo then covered his head and made his companions understand that it was time to go back on their way.

"What did he mean? Why do not you have so much time? And who was he?"

This time it was one of Tembo's companions who responded.

"Hey, you are asking too many questions, young lady! Just sit down and let it go! You cannot understand anyway."

Taken aback, Nsona did not react immediately. But facing the silence and passivity of her husband, who had nevertheless followed the scene, she got carried away.

"What?! Who are you to talk to me so?! I have every right to ask my husband any question, any time! How does that involve you?! What does that mean? Tembo! Tembo! Tembo!!"

But Tembo paid no attention to her. He had other concerns. This time it was from the front that came a troop of riders resembling in every way the former ones that had approached them. In a flash they were in front of them. This time there was no discussion. One of the men broke away from the group and came to take three of the remaining horses and their charge. He carried them before the helpless gaze of Tembo and his companions. As quickly as they had arrived, the riders left in the rain, which still had not stopped. As soon as they had disappeared, the small troop set off again at high speed. There were only seven horses left in total. Including those carrying Nsona's luggage.

The young woman had now understood that Tembo had a commitment and that he had to fulfill it in a time allotted. But why would he allow himself to be robbed of his property in this way? She no longer believed in the explanations he had given her in previous situations. What was going on? Tonight, when they would get to the next community, he would have to tell her more. She would not let herself be abandoned as he had done so far. Or else, she would be ready to find another place to spend the night.

*

They had been crossing the forest at a high pace and had left it almost when the rain had stopped. They had then continued their journey through a series of endless savannahs and bush. After their frantic cavalcade, they had finally reached another small forest in which they had engulfed without slowing down. This one housed the next step.

They finally arrived at their destination for the night. Nsona widened her eyes as she looked around. It was not at all what she expected. Her rebelliousness immediately faded. In front of her was a new house identical to those that had housed her every night. She immediately noted despite the lack of light that there was just the door as the only opening. But above all, she noted that the house was isolated in the middle of a sort of clearing. All around there were only thorny bushes of a kind she had never seen before, with almost black leaves. There was no other visible construction. Beyond the bushes, she could only see the trees, threatening like giants ready to fall on her.

"Where are we...? Tembo?"

The remark of the man earlier in the day who had rebuffed her was still in her head. But despite this she absolutely wanted her husband to answer her. She could not stay so without knowing exactly what was going on. She jumped out of her seat and walked over to him.

"Where are we, Tembo?! What are we doing here?"

The young man's companions had gathered and looked at him. They seemed curious to see what he intended to answer to her and how. But the latter remained calm, as usual.

"We are exactly where I wanted us to be for the night. So do not worry. You will be safe inside and we will be outside to stand guard."

The young woman insisted.

"You did not answer my question: where are we?"

She could not take her eyes off him. He understood that he would have to give her a more consistent answer to calm her down. He looked up and saw his companions who were still looking at him. He got off his mount and stood before her. He suddenly appeared to her to be taller and a little older than he had seemed to be since she had known him.

"We are in the heart of the forest known as the "wanderers' forest". Have you ever heard of it?"

"No."

"Tomorrow, when we shall have crossed it, we shall have made most of our journey. We shall not be very far. We cannot continue because it would be dangerous to move after dark. There are all kinds of wandering nocturnal creatures that we might come across. That is what explains this name."

A lightning followed by a sudden thunderbolt interrupted the conversation. Almost immediately, the rain began to fall profusely. The young man took the opportunity to lead the young woman towards the construction while one of his companions took care of bringing her some goods for the night. Once again she found herself alone in the dim light of the torch that the man had lit as the door closed behind her. She did not even want to lock it up. She knew it would be from outside. At the very least, Tembo and his companions would be there. She saw a table, already set. She shuddered. She knew she would not eat anything tonight. She did not know who had prepared this table nor when or how. There was no one in leagues around. So where did this food come from? She decided to lie down without even grooming. She did not have the courage. But all this did not prevent her from invoking her ancestors.

10

Day 5

"Where is the best place in the world?

"At home." Nsona replied.

"Who are we happiest with?

"With our own." she replied.

The woman drew her face closer to her, almost touching her.

"So what are you doing around here, alone and isolated?"

"But I am not alone! I am with my husband, Tembo!"

The face moved back and roared in a laughter that seemed endless to the young woman. It leaned back towards her.

"And do you really mean what you are saying? Is this man really your husband?"

She began to laugh again but with a nervous way this time. She then leaned over to the young woman and almost shouted at her.

"But why have you not understood?! Before it is too late, my child: open your eyes!"

Nsona startled. She opened her eyes and sit up on the bed. Her heart painfully hit her chest. Outside, the sound of rain was still as intense as when she had gone to bed much earlier. She heard a rolling thunder moving away. It must have burst nearby and had certainly awakened her up. The torch was off. So she had slept more than half the night. She thought of Tembo and worried for a few seconds for him. Then the dream and the words that the woman had uttered came back to her very quickly. A woman she had to consider seriously, even if it was just a dream. Her mother, the one who had given birth to her, was the one who had spoken to her in that way.

It was just a dream, she said to herself. But dreams are a way often used by the deceased to send a message to loved ones they had left. This was more than a belief; it was a certainty. So if her mother had decided to talk to her, she had a good reason to do so. A deceased person did not come to talk to you in vain. Either it was to comfort a distress and help overcome it by restoring courage, or it could to warn of a future danger. On other occasions, just after his death, the person could come forward simply to say a final farewell.

It was therefore better for her to regard this message as a serious warning. But a caveat against what? Or rather against whom? Indeed, having told her that she was with her husband had made her say that he might not be. But why? Was he not worthy of her? He had done everything he could to be so legitimately. He had introduced himself to his family and had fulfilled all the requests that the family had made and much more. He had been an unwavering supporter during the death of ma Kimani by providing moral and even material assistance when necessary. Everyone had appreciated him at the fabulous wedding ceremony he had masterfully organized. He had always been respectful of his new in-laws. So what was hidden? What was there that she did not see? Or rather that she did not want to see, if she analyzed the words made by her mother in her dream? She would have to ask Tembo a few questions.

The wind was blowing strongly. She could hear it sneaking between the trees. She thought she was hearing stray dogs howling to death. Stray? The name of the forest that Tembo had told her came back to her mind. The wanderers' forest. Why was it called so? He had spoken of creatures wandering at night, making it dangerous. What if this was still the result of a new belief? What if Tembo told her that just to dissuade her from wanting to go out in the night? Instinctively, she prepared to open the door, which she knew was locked from the outside. At least she thought so. It door opened without any effort from her. She was so surprised that she felt a chill. Nevertheless, she took a step outwards. The clearing was calm, despite the drops falling. But the trees, on the other hand, were subjected to severe stress by the wind which made them lean in one direction and then in the other. This contrast between the wind-shaken trees all around the clearing whose bushes were still was striking. But, curiously, she did not let herself be impressed. In the dark, she looked for Tembo and his companions. She saw no one on either side. Maybe there was a shelter at the back of the house? She hesitated at first. But, taking her courage in her hands, she pushed the door away and began to go around it. She walked along one of the side walls, casting in spite of herself stealthy glances at the trees that moved and seemed to be getting closer. But it was just a feeling. She arrived at the back of the small building. There was no one or anything. She continued to look around the edge of the clearing hoping to see one or more familiar silhouettes. She came back to the door without seeing anyone. She glanced one last time around and returned in. The wind was still blowing, howling between the trees. They continued their impressive broom. The clearing was always as calm, with no wind blowing. Only a few drops of rain pounded the ground loudly.

Once inside Nsona wondered what she should think of this situation. She was alone. Just as her mother had told her in her dream. Where did he go? Why did he leave her on her own after he had said he would be staying there to stand guard? Her decision was made in a blink of an eye. She was going back home. That is what her mother made her understand. She had to get back home before it was too late. She did not have a mount and she would carry the simple necessities to go fast.

*

"This just cannot be possible! No one has seen him come back? Is not there anybody who knows where he is?"

"No, there is not."

Pa Ebata then turned to the guardian of the collective memory.

"Do you confirm to me that he came to see you two days ago? Well, I do know that he did. So where did you send him?"

"I sent him to see the family of the one whose probity you doubt. I have not seen him since. He had no reason to come back here."

"By the way, why did you send him there?"

"They alone can best talk about their families. Since everything I said to your friend did not seem to satisfy him, so I sent him there. Perhaps he left Mbanza Miongo to collect information elsewhere."

"Indeed." Father Ebata said thoughtfully. "But if that had been the case, he would have warned me or had me warned."

He pretended to leave but stopped, looking at his interlocutor again.

"There is one aspect I do not understand," he said. "How is it, even if what you told him did not satisfy him, that you sent him to see the family concerned and not one of your colleagues?"

The man hesitated. He did not seem to know what to say.

"It is just that... Well.... Uh, the others do not know any more than I do."

"What do you mean?! So who gave the information that validated our child's marriage?"

This time the keeper seemed astonished.

"We never gave enough information! And all the ones we gave were conditional because we had very few references!"

"There is something that I do not understand," pa Ebata insisted. "On our side, if we had validated the marriage with this family, it is because we supposedly had all useful information to decide. So someone allowed us to make that decision. If it is not you, then who did?"

There was a strange silence.

"I do not know," the memory keeper replied. "But why did you not talk to this family before the wedding? This is also in the manners. You would have had answers to your questions!"

Pa Ebata sighed, slightly annoyed.

"We did not know at the time that there was any family of this young man who lived here."

Pa Ebata suddenly felt very anxious. The situation was very strange. He had begun his investigations after his promise to his brother Sadisa, thinking that he would settle the matter quickly, simply and unhindered. But he began to wonder if his eldest had not had a shrewdest idea when he felt like checking one last time where this suitor really came from. Today he was faced with the disappearance of a friend who had kindly agreed to help him. It was a duty for him to find him and make sure he was fine. He decided to first go to pa Sadisa before going over to Tembo's family.

His visit and the report he made to him did not reassure his eldest. On the contrary, they caused him concern that only the outcome of the coming visit could resolve. He even offered to accompany his younger brother on a more formal visit. But pa Ebata refused, saying that they lacked time to prepare for such a visit. He would go alone at first. He would pretend an impromptu visit because he would be passing around the area. It was common to visit people when close to their home. It happened very often to arrive unexpectedly at an acquaintance's place, whether it was close or not. Even if it was in-laws. When such an opportunity arose, it was necessary to take advantage of it because no one knew what the future had in store. So he left, assuring that the matter would be resolved quickly and that he would return rapidly and certainly with answers to their questions. He took almost the same route as that taken by Lukuayi the day before to get there. He was moving forward with a quick and determined step. He did not meet any acquaintances on his way. He was, however, rather well known. Maybe it was because it was getting late? There was not much time left before the sun began to decline. So he was speeding up the step so he would not arrive too late.

He arrived near the impressive construction that had been indicated to him. It was not difficult to recognize. It was the only one to be so imposing and also a little isolated from the others. He glanced around but saw no living soul. Over the tall grass that lined the fence, he looked into the inner courtyard.

There was no one in sight. He passed the entrance, casting an intrigued glance at the white flowers. He found it curious to put white flowers overlooking an entrance because white was by tradition the color of death. He entered the yard anyway. It was empty of any presence. He then saw the entrance which seemed to welcome him with open arms. He advanced up the steps. Still not seeing anyone, he called.

"Hello, is there anyone in?"

Silence answered him back. But he seemed to hear a slight noise coming from within. So he insisted.

"Is there anyone? I am Pa Ebata! I am an uncle of Nsona, the young woman your child Tembo married a short time ago!"

It was then that a voice answered him. A voice he recognized and it relieved him.

"Oh, is it you my friend Ebata? Guess what? We were waiting for you!"

Reassured, pa Ebata stepped forward and crossed the threshold of the door to try to reach that voice he had hoped to hear again. He had barely moved two steps down the hall as the opening through which he had entered began to fade. He did not notice it, busy he was trying to locate the voice. But for him, it was already too late.

The sun was just beginning to warm an atmosphere still laden with the humidity of the night's rain. The trees of the wanderers' forest were slowly moving away behind them. This time, the landscape consisted of sparse shrubs and bushes, an almost black color just like the bushes in the clearing that shed the house where Nsona had spent the night.

"What a strange setting. And what are these plants?"

The young woman had been intrigued since they had left the clearing. Everything seemed unrealistic to her. First, the way Tembo had brought her back to the house after advising her not to leave alone in the night.

"If you want to go back home, for whatever reason, it is your right. But I would not recommend that to you. I have just realized myself that the men I considered to be my companions had in fact only very personal and above all hidden goals to be with me. I cannot trust them anymore. I preferred to tell them that I no longer saw the value of their presence with us. So they left in the middle of the night. You see that it is not very nice of them to leave us so on our own in the middle of the night. That is why I myself had settled away so that I could discreetly monitor your

228

front door. So I saw you come out. That allowed me to intercept you when you came out to leave. I have to admit, you really had me scared."

Tembo had indeed caught up with his wife shortly after she had embarked on the route they had taken to reach the clearing. She had been startled when she had seen him. It did not surprise her. The dark and rainy environment explained this largely. This was the explanation he had given her to justify his absence from the house and those of his former companions to him. On her side, Nsona had explained that having not seen them, she had panicked, thus taking this foolish risk of hitting the road alone in the middle of the night in a highly stormy weather. They then had an intense discussion outside the door, Tembo still not wanting to be in a closed place with her before arriving in Mbuila. She had, however, expressed to him her grievances with his attitude, but also her incomprehension that he had gradually lost his companions and much of his property. Now he had only two mounts left, including his own, as well as Nsona's. Overall, they still had six animals that they had loaded as heavily as possible to avoid abandoning too many goods on the way. Besides, it was better not to have too many. At first it attracted attention, and there was no one left to help them if necessary.

"They are called sentinel bushes. Legend says that they are able to prevent the imminent arrival of the spirits of the deceased from your own family to do you harm."

Nsona chuckled.

"Really? And how is that possible?"

While keeping his serious attitude, Tembo replied.

"They start by rippling to one side and then on the other, after they writhe on themselves. I wish you not to see that happen."

"So if people say so, it is because it has certainly already happened?"

"I cannot tell you any more. I have never been confronted with it myself."

Nsona did not answer. They continued one in front of the other, walking at an ever-increasing pace, until they reached for a stream that had come in the way. Imperceptibly, Tembo gradually slowed down his small procession. It was as if he expected someone or something to come up. But nothing happened. Slowly, they approached the shore. Arriving just a few steps from the water they stopped. Tembo got off his mount. He approached the waters that stretched before them. Further on, a grayish patch of fog floated over the still waters.

That was what intrigued Nsona. The stream did not flow one way or the other. And if it was a lake, there was no wave that came to die on the shore. She was very uncomfortable. But she saw her husband remain totally in control of his nerves. She wondered if it was normal for him to be.

"What are we waiting for?" She asked him. "And why are we so lonely? We have not met anyone since this morning."

He turned to her, beckoning her to be quiet and listen. She obeyed, listening. Imperceptibly, a steady noise was rising from the waters. Listening carefully, she recognized the characteristic sound of oars entering the water. Slowly, a large boat emerged from the thick mist. At first, the young woman saw only a vague shape, but she ended up distinguishing one silhouette, then two. One was standing at the tip of the boat and facing them. The other was towards the back of the boat and was moving the boat forward with elegant regularity. He also faced them. They were dressed like the men they had met in the wanderers' forest: a long white cloth cape with a hood that covered their heads.

Was that an impression? Or was it suddenly darker?

"Oh, Tembo! You are finally back! We have been waiting for you for a while, already! What did you bring for me from your trip?"

Tembo waved to the arrivals with his hand.

"Get us through and you will get your due, keeper!"

Tembo had used a dry tone of voice. Almost aggressive.

Nsona did not understand because the man had been rather kind. Why such an attitude? Was there a dispute between them? He also called him a keeper. Keeper of what? At first glance, it seemed to her that he was a boatman. But the moment was not suitable to ask questions, especially since the two men had already begun to grab the mounts and load them onto the boat. The young woman wondered if all would be able to board. But that was no problem. She had the strange feeling that the boat had adapted to the loading. If she had clearly realized that it was not just a feeling, she would have certainly jumped into the water with panic.

*

When arriving on the opposite bank, the sky was hardly brighter than at the beginning. Yet it already seemed to be the beginning of the afternoon. The crossing had been long and Nsona was looking forward to this moment. She had had the opportunity to see the faces of the two boatmen and she had not found them reassuring. In fact, the way they looked at her had instead pushed her to instinctively stay as close as possible to her husband. It was from that moment that she began to regret being in these places. What had happened to her? She would never talk off the top any more. She would never again do so, despise ancestral beliefs. She would start by taking seriously what her mother had said to her. She realized that the fact that Tembo was so comfortable in these increasingly strange places gave another relief to what she had told him. She had to run away. She had failed to do so at the first try. She would do it again.

Tembo took her in his arms to bring her to the mainland, while the man who occupied the front of the boat landed the horses. He first brought down the young woman's. Then he went up to bring down those of the young man. But instead, the boat began to move away, taking away the three horses and the latter's belongings.

"Have a good way back!" the man said.

Nsona could not hold back.

"But!..?" she cried. "Tembo, Tembo! He is leaving with our belongings! Please do something!"

What was not her surprise to see the reaction that was his.

"Silence, young lady! From now on, I advise you to keep a low profile and be discreet! You are not in your world here anymore, you are in mine. Besides, you have been in it for a while now. And you had better follow my instructions! We must not be seen. Come up to your seat!"

Nsona reluctantly performed. But she still had no idea of why she should have gone home.

They set off again, but this time much slower than they had done before. Not because Tembo was on foot, but because he wanted to make as little noise as possible when they moved. He walked cautiously looking at all sides. He was obviously afraid of something, or even someone. Nsona still did not understand his attitude. But she soon knew why. The landscape had not changed from before the crossing of the river. They were always in the middle of the sentinel bushes.

*

Since she had returned the day before from Mbanza Miongo, Lukuayi had gone about her business. By the end of the afternoon she had felt unwell. She had then complained of stomach aches. Her mother-in-law had concluded that it had something to do with the young woman's pregnancy. She had simply recommended her to rest a little after ingesting an infusion. Everything would be better later. Indeed, she had felt better shortly before dark. She had then got up to finish preparing for her husband's return home. She had gone to bed without any other form of concern.

But she had slept badly and by the morning she had complained about her stomach again. Greatly worried, her husband had brought in a healer to examine her and do what was necessary to make her feel better. The man had concluded that she was very tired and had advised the young woman to rest for the day. The young woman had then lay down, following the advice of the healer, but also of many others around her. No sooner had she lay down than she had begun to feel some relief. Obviously it was the right solution.

*

Nsona and her husband arrived at the foot of a passage that separated two huge black rock faces. These extended on both sides to infinity. One obviously had to go through the opening to reach the other side. It was half a dozen steps wide. It was not possible to see the end of it because it formed a curve. There were sparse bushes, as well as shrubs and low grass. All this vegetation had an unusual dark color for plants. Nsona did not recognize any of them. She was not reassured by the gaping mouth that opened up in front of them. There was no one in sight in front or behind. The atmosphere was agonizing. But, paradoxically, the young woman told herself that as long as she stayed close to Tembo, nothing would happen to her. She still meant something to him. She did not know why, but she felt it. Nevertheless, she also knew that at the first opportunity she would have to run away. But the further they went, the more difficult it would certainly be.

"Let us go." Tembo said.

They entered the passage along the right side. As for discretion, Tembo was served because the grassy, slightly sandy soil perfectly stifled the sound of their horses' hooves. They advanced for a long time before reaching the curve which was further away than it had appeared at first. The two young brides were constantly looking up, as if a nasty surprise could fall off the rock walls. Tembo did so for reasons him alone knew, but Nsona did so more out of mimicry in relation to him.

The trajectory of the opening had changed. The sky was still as little illuminated. The sun was not even detectable under the thick layer of clouds that looked more like some kind of blanket. In this persistent darkness, a figure that stood crouched on a sort of platform dug into one of the walls appeared before the young couple. Tembo was obviously very nervous. He slowed down but continued to advance. They reached the man. The clothing was the same: a white canvas cape with a hood

"Oh, Tembo!" The man said. "Is that you?"

"You are waiting for me too, are you not?!"

"No, not me. What interest would I have in waiting for you?"

Then he looked at the young woman who was passing in front of him. She did not dare to raise her head to see his face. Once she was a few steps away, he uttered a rather neutral sentence that puzzled the young woman.

"Well, if the tree knew what the axe had in store for it, it would not provide it with the wood for its handle."

The young woman turned briefly. Why say such a sentence? Obviously it was for her. Tembo apparently did not hear this statement because he was a little further away and had not expressed any reaction. Was that another warning? She could not help but think of the proverb that the man had uttered. So what was in reserve for her? She no longer had any doubt that she was at the centre of what was going on. Yet, what was going on? Why did Tembo come to pick her up? And why her?

The passage continued on, turning sometimes in one direction, sometimes in the other. It seemed endless. The ambient light did not modify. In her estimates of the elapsed time, Nsona was convinced that it should have already been dark. She wondered how she would be able to escape. She was sure that somehow Tembo had the means to stop her. So she could only count on herself.

*

The passage snaked endlessly. It just would not come to an end. Nsona and Tembo had not spoken for a very long time. She was getting more and more tired. She was now convinced that it should have been dark a long time ago.

"Tembo," she said shyly, "when are we going to get out of this endless bottleneck?"

He did not answer. But then everything happened very quickly. From a crack in the wall that Nsona had not seen came two white silhouettes, their faces hidden by a hood."

"It is about time, Tembo!! You have abused the time we have given you to carry out your tasks. You have to give us our property back now! We need it ourselves!"

Immediately said, the shadow recovered the horse that Tembo was holding. The latter did not resist. Suddenly, other white shadows appeared and began to strip the young couple of the few goods left.

"This is mine!" one said before serving and disappearing with his loot.

"And this mine," another one said in echo before doing the same.

"And I am getting that horse back!"

"Give me that bracelet back, Tembo!"

Everything happened so quickly that Nsona did not realize the situation until she was on the ground. The horses she was travelling on from Mbanza Miongo had also been taken away. Only her personal belongings had not been taken. She then turned her eyes to Tembo. He was practically naked. He had only the piece of white cloth that he used to cover his private parts. Even his beautiful clothes had also been taken away. There was nothing left for him! He only had a beautiful hairstyle to parade with. Very useless for the situation. He seemed ridiculous.

While the young woman was still trying to regain her spirits and understand what had just happened, he picked up the few straps that had fallen from the undone luggage in the hustle and tied her hands and feet. Then he lifted her like a simple bundle of straw on his shoulder, revealing an unsuspected strength.

"I have nothing to hide or lose now!" he said with new vigor in his voice. "So we are going to keep moving, without wasting any time!"

"But what does that mean? Let me go! Who are you? Release me, Tembo or whoever you are!!"

But Tembo was no longer listening. He had started running. Obviously time was playing against him. On his shoulders, she did not seem to weigh more than a simple packet of feathers. He had reached a cruising pace and was proceeding at a regular and steady rhythm. As for Nsona, she saw the ground flash along before her eyes, helpless.

11

The walls were still present on both sides. Tembo did not seem to ever weaken. Nsona said to herself that she had to try something. She had the opportunity to loosen her hands with her teeth. Tembo could not see her do it. So she took advantage of it. Once she had her hands free, she hugged the legs of her abductor; as for her now he was one. Tembo fell, head forward. She was thrown a few steps ahead of him. She stood up and began to loosen her feet while Tembo raised his head from the ground. She freed herself as he rose slowly, looking at her with anger in his eyes.

Nsona found him completely changed. He no longer had his youthful air that had seduced and attracted her. It even seemed to her that he had suddenly taken a few more years of age. Refusing to get closer to him, she started running in the wrong direction, thus continuing the journey they had begun towards what was for her the unknown. She kept running as fast as she could, remembering the crazy races she used to perform as a child with her best friend, Lukuayi. This thought gave her extra energy. She turned back to see where Tembo was. She saw him begin to run painfully while holding his shoulder. She accelerated. She had to hide somewhere. But the passage did not end and the walls were too high to be climbed. So she had to go straight ahead, always straight ahead.

Suddenly, she seemed to hear the crying of a baby in front of her. Finally, she was going to be able to take refuge with someone. If there was baby crying, it was because there was definitely a family. A woman would not travel alone with a baby. There should be at least two adults. They could protect her from Tembo. She accelerated her race even further. She began to see a white shadow sitting on a rock at the edge of the passage. Obviously, this outfit was an obligation in the vicinity, she thought. She would certainly need to have one to be a little more unnoticed. She slowed down as the child's crying became louder. They came from the arms of the woman who was sitting with her head bowed down. As she drew closer, she distinguished the voice of the woman who was singing.

"My child, do not cry
Living was not for you
My child, do not cry
This world is all you will know
My child, do not cry
Forgive me, I did not know
My child, do not cry

Please do not blame me"

In her enthusiasm, Nsona laid her hands on the lady who raised suddenly her head towards her. The hood that covered her head fell backwards, revealing a sad face marked by intense pain. The young woman startled strongly back.

"Lukuayi?!" she exclaimed. "But...! What are you doing here?"

Her best friend looked at her. She did not seem to understand Nsona's question. Or even why she asked her.

"What am I doing here? The question should be what are you doing here. I belong here. But do you? Your time has not arrived yet, Nsona!"

Nsona recoiled, greatly frightened. She did not want to understand.

"What do you mean by saying you belong here?"

The baby had become silent. He was looking at Nsona.

"Nsona, you are going in the wrong direction! If you get out of this passage on the side you are heading to, it will be forever! So go back! Go home before it is too late! Go back the other way!!"

"But !..."

"Forget Songo! Forget Mbuila! You are never going to make it. In any case, this is not the right way. This man does not want you any good! Since you left Nzila Kumi, you are in a place you do not belong to!"

"But what does that mean?!.."

Nsona had become almost hysterical. Lukuayi continued.

"Just turn around and go home!"

The child began to cry again.

"My child, don't cry
  Living was not for you
  My child.... "

Nsona looked back to see where Tembo was. He was getting closer. She started running again. But she continued in the same direction as before. She was now getting tired. How long was she going to be able to escape from him? And this passage that never ended! At the bend of a curve, she suddenly felt lifted into the air as if she was sort of absorbed by one of the walls. She found herself in a sort of cave in which there was a group of people in white capes with a hood. She turned to the person who had forcibly dragged her there. The latter pointed his finger at her to have her look behind her. Once more, she startled.

"Nsona, my child, many times you have had warnings that you have not been able to obey. But today, you are going to have to do exactly what I am going to tell you."

"Pa Ebata? But what are you also doing around here? And I still do not understand what Lukuayi is doing here!"

"Listen to me! All you have to do is get out of here. There is a horse waiting for you. You ride it and you go home. Do you hear me? You are going back home. Your time has not come. Go!"

"But..."

"Go! Do not delay! Time is running out!! Go!!"

He beckoned one of those who were with him to push her immediately outwards. She came out of the crack in the wall in which she had been swept away and found herself shivering with fright in the passage. She saw a white shadow coming towards her. One more, she thought to herself. But it took her delicately by the hand and then lifted her on a horse whose presence she had not noticed right next to her. There was a beautiful wicker saddle on which she settled in a sidesaddle position. For a moment, she caught a glimpse of the man's face. She thought she recognized a friend of her uncle whom she had just seen. She had no time to wonder what he was doing there too. He struck the rump of the horse, which gradually shook until it reached a speed at which she had become accustomed to during the long journey. She quickly returned to the location where she had seen Lukuayi earlier: her friend was no longer there. However, it made her think that she was going in the right way because she had also lost all sense of direction. She hoped Tembo would go far before returning back after her. Also, unlike her, he had no mount. But she knew he could move very fast. On the other hand, if she had been able to get a horse, he maybe would be able to do the same.

She went back through the whole route. It turned on one side and then on the other, depending on the path of the passage. Oddly enough, she felt that it was reducing as she progressed. The walls seemed to be getting closer. She began to observe the endless walls more closely. They were much less wider than when she entered with her husband. Was that why his uncle said time was running out? She pushed her mount to accelerate, thinking that there would be no big difference because it was already speeding greatly. She was surprised to feel the horse go even faster. So one should never really doubt. She had to hang on as much as she could so as not to fall.

She finally arrived at sight of the entrance, with the sentinel bushes in the background. She was relieved when she found herself in the middle of them. She glanced back to see if she was being followed by anyone, but she saw nothing. She then felt the horse slowing down abruptly. She looked ahead. The horse stopped. She glanced around her but saw no living soul.

"Why do you stop? What is going on? Come on! Come on!"

But the animal did not move one step.

"He will not move," a voice said.

Nsona shuddered. She did not see the person who had uttered the words. She looked at the bushes around her. In vain.

'Who's horse is this?"

"My uncle gave it to me."

"Which uncle?"

"Papa Ebata."

There was a long silence. The young woman was shaking. She could not see who she was talking to. There was no one around. In any case, she did not see anyone.

"We do not know him. Who are you?"

She was terrified.

"I am Nsona, daughter of papa Sadisa and mama Kimani.

There was a new silence.

"We do not know either of these!"

"But who are you, finally?! And what do you want from me?"

Silence again. Nsona tried again to move the horse forward. With no result. The animal still was not moving.

"Can you explain how you ended up on this beast whereas you are not one of us?"

"But I just told you!" the young woman exasperated. "My uncle gave it to me!"

"An uncle we do not know. So tell us the name of someone we know."

"You certainly know Lukuayi, she is in the passage with her baby. She is my best friend."

"With a baby, you say?"

She waited for a while that seemed endless to her.

"No, we do not know her either. It is still amazing that this beast lets you ride it. It is like if it does not know you are not from here."

"Oh,.. Oh, right? Only those from here can ride the mounts from here?"

"Oh yes!" several voices answered in chorus.

Nsona frantically looked around her. But she still did not see anyone. She was also unable to say whether the voices were female or male.

"In any way, if you do not know anyone from here, we will not let you through."

"Oh, ma Myezi," the young woman sobbed."Come to my aid!"

"Who did you say?"

"Ma Myezi, she was the one who gave birth to me."

"But then, who is ma Kimani? Would you have lied to us?"

The voice was threatening. Nsona felt her will leaving her.

"Certainly not, ma Kimani is the one who raised me."

A new silence set in. Then the voice became a little more sympathetic.

"Ah, ma Myezi is from here! She has been with us for many years now!!"

"What do you mean by that?" Nsona exclaimed. "She died when I was a child!"

The horse had started galloping again. Once again, she would not have an answer to any of her questions. But doubt was gradually beginning to be instilled in her head. Maybe she had already understood, but she did not want to admit it. She did not want to recognize it. She did not want to admit it. For if she admitted it, then it would mean that she had married.... No, it could not be possible! But then who had spoken? How could the presence of Lukuayi and pa Ebata be explained? What about his friend's? How could they have found themselves in front of her after such a long journey when she had advanced at an extraordinary pace? And her mother. What was her mother doing here? It was the presence of the latter that threw a huge disturbance in her mind.

Her horse was moving as fast as it could, she did not have to push it. Obviously, it knew where it had to go. What she knew now was that she no longer had any control over him. The river was soon in sight. She arrived on the bank and began to wait, nervously scrutinizing the mist that floated over the still waters. She expected to see the boat with both silhouettes at any moment. She stretched out her ear as Tembo had done when they had passed together. Besides, what was becoming of him? She had turned around several times but had not seen a single sign of his presence behind her. Had he given up pursuing her and getting her back?

"Who are you? What are you doing here?"

Once again, Nsona thought her heart was going to stop. She looked for where the voice that had just addressed her came from. And again, she could not say whether it was a woman or a man. For a short moment, she could not see anyone. She answered mechanically.

"I am waiting for the boat to cross."

"The boat? What boat? There has never been any boat here."

"But!.. I crossed not long ago with my husband when we were going the other way. We crossed on a boat with our horses."

"Your husband? Who is your husband?"

"His name is Tembo."

Nsona was surprised by her ability to be able to say so easily that Tembo was still her husband. After answering, she waited for the voice to react. It rang after a moment of silence.

"Ah, Tembo! But where is he? Why are you on your own?"

The young woman did not know what to say. She dared not say that she had escaped from him. Maybe she would be stuck so he could catch up with her? But what could she say?

"Did you escape from him?"

The question was direct and called for an immediate response. Nsona was stuck. Should she lie? Was it necessary to tell the truth?

"Yes, I ran from him! And I am very happy about that!"

A thick swirl of dust rose abruptly. When it dissipated a trio of old women appeared. They slowly approached her. The young woman wondered what was going to happen to her.

"You are brave", the nearest one said. "Bragging yourself out of having escaped your husband is not very smart."

She spoke slowly in a very soft voice, looking at her intensely. Nsona could not sustain her gaze. She looked away.

"Or it is unconscious," the second one said, sneering with a rocky voice.

The young woman's gaze turned to her. It was not more convenient to look at her in the eyes. She looked mechanically at the third one who was a little further back. She found the same intensity in her eyes. Black eyes and no particular emotion. In their big white tunics, however, they did not seem to mean any harm on her.

"Nsona, daughter of Myezi," the third woman said. "What are you doing here? Your time has not come yet. But we can fix that. Sometimes there are unforeseen expectations.”

“My time for what?! I do not understand what you are saying!”

She burst into tears, nerves tensed, holding her face in her hands. The horse was still motionless as the three women approached. She was frozen with fear again.

“Of course you do understand! You just do not want to admit it!”

The first woman was almost angry. The second approached, ready to touch her. It was then that the third intervened, holding her arm.

“No, wait! Let us give her a chance. She is brave enough and she deserves it.”

“Yes, the second one sneered. Let us give her an enigma to resolve. But which one?”

They were silent as they looked at each other. Then the second old woman sneered again as she looked at the first one.

“Yes, you are right! Since we are at the water's edge let us lay her one that is related to water.”

“Will you be quiet!” The third one lectured to her. “You are about to give her some clues.”

The second sneered even louder.

"You are joking! She will never find out. By the way, let me remind you that she is mine, eh! It is my turn this time! Ha! Ha! Ha!"

She began to dance frantically with excitement, wriggling her hips. The other two looked at her, unfazed. Then the first woman approached Nsona and spoke to her in her soft, suave voice.

"If you find the answer to this riddle, you can leave. The horse will take you where you need to go. Otherwise..."

"If I do not, what is going to happen to me?"

A new sneer rang out.

"You will see!"

"To climb on me, you have to go down. But to get off from me you have to climb on me. Who am I?"

Nsona was speechless. She looked up at the sky, as if seeking help. But it still looked grey and dark. There was not even a little glimmer that would have given her some hope. So what was going to happen to her once the time was up and she did not answer? What did that old sneering woman keep in store for her? And who were they anyway? Where did they come from and what were they doing here in the middle of nowhere? But did it matter?

She bowed her head and her whole life began to scroll through her head. First her childhood was a long time ago, even before ma Myezi left her unwillingly. She remembered the moments spent with her. Strangely they were more than ever present in her mind at this very special moment. She could see herself in her arms as she cradled her tenderly. She remembered the advice she had already begun to give her very early when she was just beginning to talk. She even invited her to come and help her as soon as she started an activity where she could learn something. The only time she would never let her approach was when she was going to draw water from the well at the bottom of the concession. It was too dangerous and she was right. She told him that even though she already knew how to climb trees a little, if she had fallen into it and had not drowned, she would never be able to climb up anyway. So she listened to her and never approached the well, reluctantly. She remembered the first words she had taught her. Sweet words such as love, friendship, wisdom or respect.

She suddenly realized that the basis of her upbringing came from the five years she had spent with the mother who had given birth to her, reinforced by that of the mother who had raised her. Two mothers. How lucky she had been. Two mothers who had loved her...

"A well!! You are a well!

She felt the horse start gradually as usual. He headed to the side, along the water side before turning abruptly and entering a bridge that had just risen from the mist that covered the water. It walked away as the angry howl of the old woman she was said to have been the victim of was heard behind her. Very quickly, the horse was launched at a very high speed. Visibility did not go beyond a few steps, but it did not slow down. The mist prevented Nsona from seeing far, but what about the animal? Maybe he saw beyond that? She preferred to think that was the case. The bridge was nothing more than planks assembled without railings or ledges of any kind. If the horse deviated to one side or the other, it would fall into the water without any obstacles. But she was not overly concerned. She was convinced that this would not happen.

During the boat ride, time had seemed very long, but Nsona thought that the horse was going much faster. She would certainly be on the opposite bank very quickly. She was beginning to feel a fatigue as if she had not slept for more than a day. Her eyelids were mechanically closing. Only the jolts of the gallop brought her back to awakening. She was finally going to be able to go home. What a relief. She would have a lot to tell her best friend. The picture then came back to her mind. Lukuayi with her baby in her arms, sitting at the edge of the passage. How was that possible? She could not have had her baby so fast! Her pregnancy was barely visible when she had left her a few days earlier. And above all, how could she be present in the vicinity before her? What was this place?

"Of course you understand! You just do not want to admit it! »

This sentence had been addressed to her by one of the old women. It was still bumping in her head. She began to analyze all the situations she had had to face. She remembered all the characters she had seen, including pa Ebata and his friend. But she also remembered all the riders and people in white hooded capes. Who were they? She did not want to believe it. It could not be possible! So they really existed? Belief said true? But her relatives she had seen were wearing the same clothing. But did that mean that it was also over for them?

"What are you doing here? Your time has not come!"

This meant only one thing: theirs was. But then how was it that she had arrived here when her time had not yet arrived. Was she dreaming? The fatigue she felt confirmed that she did not. Even if she had been asleep, with the one she felt she could not have dreamed. What had happened so that three of the people closest to her had died in such a short delay after her departure? Was she the origin of it? What had she done? Or rather what had she done again? For she also thought of the death of the young Sambu for whom she felt guilty in spite of herself. However, there could not be a connection.

"Who has allowed you to cross?"

She startled once more. Caught in her thoughts and weakened by fatigue, she did not realize that the horse had slowed down and even stopped. She was tired. She thought she would still hear the same questions and waste precious time. She could not see the riverbank. Barely could she see a few steps forward and a few steps backwards. Everything else was just mist. How far was it from the end of the crossing?

She bowed her head with exhaustion, spite and exasperation.

"Three old women let me through. I am Nsona, child of ma Myezi, ma Kimani and pa Sadisa. I come from Mbanza Miongo and I went to Mbuila with my husband, Tembo. But circumstances have driven me to want to go home because I am not in my world and my time has not come. I knowthat! Leave me alone! Leave me alone! I just want to go home!"

Again, there was silence as she waited for the voice to harass her with another question. But nothing happened. She finally opened her eyes. Then she saw him. It was him. Like everyone else, he wore a white canvas cape with a hood. On the other hand, she instantly distinguished his face and shivered.

"I do not understand," she stammered.

"It is easy to understand. You just have to accept the evidence. You are in the other world. You know very well that I have left yours. And you should not be here. Your uncle has already told you. Lukuayi also told you. You have not gone yet. You still have some obstacles and if you do not have anyone to accompany you it will be very difficult.

"So please, Sambu, come with me. Stay with me."

The young man looked at her. He looked sorry.

"You know I would be happy to do so, but I cannot go beyond my element. And my element is water. In the water, I can intervene for you. In the water I can protect you. But on earth I cannot do anything for you."

"Why are you stopping me? Should you not have let me go on instead of delaying me? I have also been told that I do not have much time."

He looked at her without saying anything. Then he placed himself at the edge of the bridge.

"Come with me," he said.

"What do you mean by that?"

"If you continue on this horse to the end of this bridge, then that is where your route will stop. Those who are waiting for you do not want you to go on."

He jumped into the water. Silently. There was not a single lapping from the water. It arrived up to his shoulders. He invited her with his arms to do the same. The young woman hesitated. She looked at the water with a fearful expression. Then she looked at him. He tried to reassure her.

"You know, we have known each other since childhood and I loved you like I never could have loved anyone else. But you made your choice to say no to me. I told you I did not blame you. Remember? I could not blame you, just for love. So tell me why I should want to hurt you now?"

Should she trust him? Was she really expected at the end of the bridge to prevent her from passing and going home? How could she be sure? She could not, but it was plausible. If there had been someone to prevent her from crossing, there might also be someone to block her access to the bank. On the other hand, she remembered his words on the day of his death and it touched her. He certainly knew that he was about to die but had shown no hostility towards her. Until now, the people she had known and whom she had seen again had come to her aid. So why not Sambu too?

"I do not know how to swim," she said fearfully.

"The water is coming to my shoulders. I am not much taller than you are, so I do not think it is going to be necessary. But do not jump. You would make noise."

He held out his arms again. She approached, looking at the water that seemed darker than ever. He took her by the hips and let her sink slowly into the still liquid. The water rose gently along her body to her neck as her feet reached the bottom. He smiled tenderly and began to train her with him. He did not move either side of the bridge, but walked away from it along the length of the stream.

"Where are you taking me?" she asked with a concern in her voice.

"We shall get as far away from the bridge as possible to avoid any unpleasant surprises when returning to shore."

He continued to move forward with fluidity that she found extraordinary. But was she not having extraordinary moments? Who would believe her if she ever had the opportunity to tell anyone about it?

The water was cold. Again, she noted how quickly they were moving. So everyone could move at incredible speeds in this world? She thought they had travelled far enough to be able to land safely.

"Why do you continue in this direction? Have we not gone far enough yet?"

Everything happened very quickly. He started by talking to her.

"I told you I loved you. That is not exactly the truth. In fact I still love you. I want you to stay with me."

"What do you mean by that?"

"Your time has finally arrived," he said softly." You are going to join me forever."

She then felt the ground slip under her feet. He took her suddenly by the shoulders and began to drag her with him underwater. She had sunk before she had even realized what was going on. She tried to wrestle, but he was far too strong for her. She began to run out of air. She swallowed a sip of water, then a second one. Gradually, she was no longer aware of anything.

12

"Nsona, my child! Nsona, wake up! Please sober up!"

She seemed to be dreaming. The voice she heard seemed far away. However, it seemed familiar to her. Then she heard another one that seemed equally familiar to her, but which did not reassure her.

"Nsona, please wake up. We are running out of time."

She slowly opened her eyes and saw what she dreaded. She jumped up and suddenly straightened up on her buttocks. She tried to back off with her hands to get away from the one she least wanted to see and dreaded the most. The latter tried to reassure her.

"No, I am no longer the one you have known. Do not be afraid."

He was trying to lean towards her.

"No! I have all reasons to fear from you! I do not even know you!! I do not even know who you are!"

Tembo then stood up, casting a disgruntled look over Nsona's shoulder. He shook his head in spite. The young woman felt a presence manifest behind her back. She felt a kind of well-being though she had no idea who or what it was. The voice reassured her.

"He is telling the truth, my child. You have nothing to fear from him. To tell you the truth, his interest now is to make sure that you go home safely. Otherwise it would cost him."

She turned to convince herself that the voice that spoke to her belonged to the one she was thinking of. She was not surprised to see ma Myezi. But at her side was also ma Kimani. Both seemed relieved to see her regain consciousness. She tried to throw herself into their arms, but they waved to her to guard ability.

"We are of the same blood," ma Kimani said," even symbolically. Making physical contact would not be without consequences. Especially for you. That is why you have to trust Tembo. He is going to come with you on your way back. You will have some obstacles in your way, but he will do whatever it takes to succeed. We asked him to."

"How did you get him to agree to do the complete opposite of what he has done so far?"

Ma Myezi leaned towards her.

"He had a mission to accomplish: to bring you back within a time limit to the city of ancestors. He failed. He will be punished no matter what, because everything he has done has had indirect consequences. But this punishment will be balanced if he brings you home safely."

Nsona then turned to Tembo.

"But why me? What is so special about me? Why did you want to take me to this city?"

It was ma Kimani who answered.

"My child, we have done everything for you during our living time. We tried to instill in you what we felt was the best way to behave."

Ma Myezi then spoke.

"But there is one thing we could not do anything about, and that is your personality. We are responsible for your education, but you are solely responsible for what you choose to do with it."

"And it seems that you have, in the eyes of some, neglected one of our five traditional virtues a little too much. There have been some unfortunate and exceptional initiatives that have led to the situation we are in now."

"Fortunately, we have rules that allow disputes to be resolved without conflict. So everything is back to normal but there are still some opponents to the normalization of this case and who do not want to see you return from here. That is why you need an escort and it is the one who brought you here who has to get you out."

"Yes", ma Kimani concluded. "To him it is a necessity. Life seems definitive here and it is better to avoid certain punishments because they can last... an eternity. Here we do not age, we normally do not rejuvenate. We just exist. We are waiting for the rest. The decision of God."

There was a sudden silence. Nsona gave a circular look. They were on the bank of the river. Beyond the shore, the sentinel bushes spread as far as the eye could see. No sound came from the water nor the earth. Many questions jostled in the young woman's head.

"What about Sambu?"

Ma Kimani sighed.

"Sambu was opportunistic. He will be punished for his act."

"He is not a bad boy," she argued.

"That is right. But for all that, he must answer to the community for what he has done or tried to do. God help him."

Nsona laid eyes on her two mothers. The former had the physical form she had when she died. Young and beautiful. It was the memory she had of her. A memory that was forever etched in her. She had not changed. She was impressed by how much she had kept her mother's features in herself. As for ma Kimani, her passing was still fresh. She found a melancholy in her attitude and in her gaze. Had she not gotten used to her new fate yet?

"How did you know I was here?"

"Everything is quickly known when someone from the other world comes to visit us. But it is mostly that Tembo was not far behind you. He had already understood what his fate would be after his failure and he asked us to help him. He knew we would not refuse. We arrived just in time. In fact, we were waiting for you at the end of the bridge. Sambu had lied to you."

"How is it that some of you are known and not others? The old women I met only knew you, mama Myezi."

"Those who are known have been here long enough to be. The others have either recently arrived or still have the opportunity to leave."

"Do you receive a lot of visits from the other world?"

Mother Myezi had a small smile.

"Much more than you can imagine. They are usually unconscious people who do not pay attention to who they are dating or what they are doing. And if by misfortune they open a door with imprudent words, just as you did, then they quickly find themselves here provided an ill-intentioned spirit went by and heard them. There are also those who may represent an obstacle to the evil spirit designs that may be."

"Do they all go back?"

"Oh no, my child! Certainly not. The only ones who go back are those who get help from their own and only if their time has not arrived. For this, they must have invoked them regularly by the grace of the almighty. If you forget yours, they forget you too. You must know we disappear, but we do not to die. We only go to asleep. Your solicitations wake us up."

The young woman hesitated, but still resolved to ask the question that burned her lips.

"Why is not papa here?"

"All you need to know is that he is always by your side. Why do you not put on that tunic and go with Tembo?"

She gave her a whole white tunic, similar to the ones they were wearing themselves, which she put on over her wet clothes. Two horses had appeared out of nowhere, as usual. They were dark in color. Tembo had her mount on the first animal and then did the same on the second. No sooner had they settled than the two mounts began to gallop through the bushes without even letting Nsona have time to say goodbye to her mothers. They zigzagged like butterflies twirling in the wind. Exhausted as she was, Nsona had trouble holding on to her mount.

"Are we not going back to the route we used when we came?"

"It is too far away. Sambu made you drift well downstream. We are going to cut through the bushes to catch our way to the shortest. This will bring us closer to the wanderers' forest."

*

They arrived at the last house where Nsona had spent the night. He made her get down.

"You will spend the night here. Tomorrow we will leave at dawn."

"I do not even know if this is day or night anymore. I feel like I have lived a very long night since we left these places."

"Exactly the equivalent of three days of your world. This explains the exhaustion you feel. So take advantage of it to get some rest. You have been very strong. You have nothing to fear in this house. You can rest there."

He opened the door for her and waited for her to come in and close it behind her. She found herself alone again in a place she had fled some time before.

She spotted everything she found there every time. There was a bed, a set table, clean clothes that she recognized as her own. She prepared to grim. She poured lukewarm water over her body, taking her time by emptying her mind. She savored these moments before going to dress for the night and sit at the table that awaited her. She began to eat without any apprehension. Seeing her two mothers had given her a confidence she had thought she would never have regain since shad realized what she was going through.

Slowly she began to think again. She thought of the words she had exchanged with her mothers. She was thinking about why she ended up there. She remembered the reckless remarks she had made while she was with Lukuayi. So that was the trigger? No, there was something else. Her behavior was also a factor. They had told him about the five traditional virtues to be respected. Which one had she flouted?

Truth? She had lied when she had said she knew Tembo, but everything had gone off before that. And it was not in her habit to lie or disguise the truth. The circumstances that had led her to this situation were very special.

Justice? Nothing in all she thought of made her imagine that she could have caused any injustice.

Moreover, she owed nothing to anyone who could demand justice.

Kindness? Throughout her life, she had always tried to do good around herself whether by helping or avoiding conflict. Nor did she hesitate to share what she had if necessary.

Love? She had always spread it around her. With her loved ones, family or not. Was it wrong of her not to have been able to love any of all those who had shown up to marry her? It was certainly not about that love.

Wisdom? She had always listened to her parents since childhood, without making any scandal - if the word was not too strong - in anything. She had always tried to apply their teachings.

So what did they mean? They had said that "some" had felt that she had flouted one of the traditional virtues. Who were they? Were they the ancestors of the suitors she had turned away? There was no lie in her attitude. She did not want them and she had said it. She did not see how this would have led to an injustice. Was refusing to sacrifice herself by accepting someone who did not suit her a lack of kindness? Certainly not. She felt no attraction to them. It was not her fault. Perhaps she had been dilettante on some occasions, careless towards visitors in her attitude? Perhaps dismissive too, even contemptuous? Was it a lack of wisdom?

She finished her meal, got up, and then walked to the bed. She sat down and by the light of the only torch in the room, thanked her ancestors for taking care of her and begged them to continue to do so by the grace of the almighty.

*

Day 8

A door slam woke her up. She sat up on the bed. The door was wide open. There was wind coming into the room. The torch had gone out and it was dark. She had locked the door; she was almost certain. But she still had a doubt. She got up and began to approach cautiously the opening that seemed to call her. When they had arrived, the wind had been blowing through the trees beyond the clearing. This time it was also blowing in the clearing and she found it strange. But despite this she wanted to go and see what was going on. As she was about to set foot outside, the door began to close on its own. She barely had time to take a step back as it slammed. What did all the wind mean? And why did Tembo not intervene? She assumed that he had not found it necessary, but that he was well on the lookout nearby.

She came back to lie down after taking care of locking the door and make sure once and for all that it was okay. There was still a point that intrigued her and which she had forgotten the meaning of. She could still ask Tembo what it was. He would certainly have an answer. She closed her eyes. This amazing episode had not dented her serenity and confidence. She was convinced that nothing could happen to her any more. On the one hand because Tembo's presence was an undeniable asset for her, but mainly because she knew that she was being cared for. She fell again in a deep sleep.

*

Gentle knocks at the door woke her up again. She listened.

"Nsona, it is time to go!"

It was Tembo. He came to wake her up. She got up quickly, prepared her few belongings—she did not have many left —and went out. She saw then that there were the two horses with all her luggage that she had lost. There were also those with the mounted seat on which she had arrived.

"This baggage is yours. There was no reason why they should not be returned to you."

"What about all those who have been stolen from you?"

Tembo looked away.

"Nothing has been stolen from me," he said in an unintelligible voice.

"Pardon me?"

"Nothing was stolen from me! All the goods that were recovered belonged to those who recovered them. I borrowed everything to make a good face in your world."

"Oh, that is it! You did look good! What a grand wedding! Food for the whole city, even for strangers and vagrants."

"The strangers and the vagrants were from here. Just like the waiters and many dancers. So you will understand that it was not difficult to feed stalls that had for real only what people wanted to see."

He made her go up and settle down. They set off and immediately found themselves among the impressive trees of the wanderers' forest. The wind was always blowing as much.

"Who are the so-called wanderers who gave their name to this forest, who exactly are they?"

"They are those who are not worthy to live in the city of ancestors. They must undergo penance in order to gain access to it. Generally they have committed misdeeds and are condemned to wander there."

Nsona was silent for a moment and then asked a new question.

"What kind of wrongdoing?"

Tembo hesitated. But he finally answered.

"There are many kinds of misdeeds that lead to the wanderers' forest. But the most common is the mischief that causes some to commit harm while thinking only of what themselves want."

"Selfishness in a way."

"Yes. Often, when you think only of yourself, you do not care about the consequences on others. And they are sometimes priceless and above all irreparable."

He was silent. Nsona felt that he still needed to express himself. She was silent and waited. Soon after he continued.

"In fact, it is a vicious circle from which it is very difficult to escape. We want something, we get it and we say to ourselves: why not more? And it starts again with the same dilemma every time: wanting more and more. Then it increases until we are ready for anything to achieve our goals despite the negative effects around us. All we think about is going further and further, leaving nothing to others and this applies to all topics. So that you will find wanderers of all origins. But it is better not to meet them. They are not always in a very sociable mood."

"Not surprising, from selfish people!"

"Yes, but it is the wandering that makes them that way."

"Oh!..Ah! So are they to be complained for?"

Silence set.

"That is where you are going to be, is it not? Are you going to be a wanderer?"

"Yes, and I am lucky to have had this proposal from yours to redeem myself somewhat of my act. It could have been even worse if I had had to go to the mountains of the condemned. I could have ended up in the inert river, too. There it is...."

"I do not want to hear more! Please!"

He looked at her. She had lowered her head and watched the ground unfold under the horses' hooves. She was thinking about herself. She was thinking about what would have been reserved for her if Tembo had succeeded in his mission. She thought it was better not to know. It was not her world. The trees kept moving with the wind that calmed down from time to time before blowing even more, rushing between the trees like an invisible inhabitant of the place.

"You need to know that everything you see in this forest will not always be what you see."

"What do you mean by that?"

"Trees can be trees, not trees, but trees. And sometimes something else, visible or invisible, an element of nature or not. Anything can be a wanderer."

"You mean that strays have the ability to take any natural form?"

He looked at her with a mysterious little smile without saying anything. She shuddered as she looked around with a fearful air.

"Do not be afraid", he reassured her. "No one can go for you other than your family. Now, your family is with you. All you can fear is not having enough time to leave here. So those who resent you will try to delay you, in one way or another."

He stopped talking, encouraging his mount to move even faster.

"What would your reward have been if you had succeeded?"

The young man looked at her.

"By the end of this journey, I do not know if you will understand, but at least you will know why I had this weakness."

He stopped his mount and beckoned Nsona to stop. That was worthless. In an instant they were surrounded by half a dozen menacing white capes. One part stood in front of them and the other behind. One of them approached, addressing Tembo directly.

"She must stay!" he said, pointing to Nsona with an accusing finger. "You promised us, Tembo!"

"You know very well that I have failed and that I already have a punishment to do! So I was freed from that promise! Now, let us through!"

The man hesitated before resuming.

"I do not care if you are free of your promise! It is up to those who have freed you! As for us you are always indebted! Indebted to us!!"

He still pointed his finger at her.

"She is not going to leave!"

"Enough talking!" Tembo cried out."Get out of our way!"

He threw his horse ahead and galloped off, dragging Nsona's horses in his wake. The three men in front of him moved off with inhuman agility. Once past, Nsona turned to see what they were doing. There was no one left.

“Where are they?” she cried out to Tembo.

“They are everywhere!! They are everywhere!”

He pushed his mount to the max as the wind became more and more violent. Trees began to pitch on one side and then on the other. The leaves flew away and obstructed their vision. But the horses seemed to be unable to be slowed down at all. Yet they were stopped by uprooted trees that fell smashed down their way.

Tembo's horse stumbled and collapsed, taking the young man with him to the ground. He violently struck a branch with his head. He remained spread out for the count. Nsona found herself alone in the middle of the tornado as the passage was blocked. She did not have time to think about anything.

“Who are you?”

Once again, Nsona looked around. Once again she did not see anyone. She looked at Tembo's inert body and had a moment of panic.

“You have to let me go!” she cried. “You have no right to detain me!”

“And what right do you have, you who are not in your place?”

Again, she was unable to define whether the voice was female or male.

"I am the daughter of ma Myezi and pa Ogada, ma Kimani and pa Sadisa! I have been allowed to go back home!"

A long silence settled.

"We do not know pa Sadisa. We only know the others. Do you have a fourth person to nominate us? It will be useful for us to let you go or not. Because here it is us who decide."

"I also know Lukuayi and pa Ebata!"

A new silence.

"We know par Ebata."

Nsona felt some relief overwhelm her.

"Where are you going?"

The voice was different from the previous one. This worried the young woman and the relief faded. She decided to keep a low profile.

"I am going back home to Mbanza Miongo."

"What did you come here for?"

The young woman narrated her incredible adventure, from her marriage to her escape in the passage, through her hostage-taking by Sambu and finally explaining how they had been stopped a few moments earlier by half a dozen quite hostile individuals.

"How can you explain that our place of residence is so disturbed? We may be wandering, but we are peaceful."

"I do not know!"

"Are you not responsible for that?"

"No! How could I have such power? I am not even from here!"

"Oh yes, we do know you are not from here. Not yet..."

This last statement did not reassure the young woman. She was not wrong. She waited again. There was a silence that contrasted with the din that preceded their cavalcade and the heavy fall of the trees. She barely could distinguish the sky, but from the little she could see, it still seemed as grey to her.

"Surely you are not responsible, but you are the only one we have here and as we have been disturbed, someone must answer for it. So it is going to be you. From now on, you will wander these places for having been the cause of the interruption of these lives."

"But what lives? I did not kill anyone!"

The voice sneered.

"And what do you think these trees are? These are lives you have taken away!"

"But it is not me! It is not me..."

She began to sob. She was out of her nerves again. Now it all started again. All the trust she had accumulated lately had completely disappeared. Why did hers abandon her?

"It doesn't matter. You are the origin of all this."

There was a long silence during which she tried to move her horse forward, without success.

"Good! We have deliberated because there are some among us who take pity on you. So we are going to give you a chance to save yourself."

It had been a new voice that had spoken. How many were they?

"You can leave on one condition: you have to answer a question we are going to ask you. If you prove unable to give us an answer that pleases us, then you will remain forever in the midst of these trees. And no one will ever be able to do anything for you. Not even yours. Because if you are here, it is also because you have your responsibilities. You are entitled to only one answer. Are you ready?"

Nsona did not answer. She was terrified. What was she going to ask him? The question came abruptly, in a cavernous and mocking voice.

"All of us present to him. All others he sees, but never me. Who am I?"

The poor girl felt a severe pain in her head. She wobbled and nearly collapsed from her mount. But something told her that if she ever fell, nothing would be possible any more for her. As long as she was up and conscious, she had a chance. She then forced herself to think, but a noise startled her and she turned around. A young girl in white clothing stood a few steps away from her. She raised her finger and pointed it at the trees.

"Do you see the white bush over there?" she said.

Nsona nodded her head when she saw the only white bush a hundred steps away.

"I am going to walk up to it. You will have to give the answer when I get back to you."

Having said so, she set off at a slow but rhythmic pace. Nsona thought to herself that she did not have much time. Time. Always that parameter that kept coming back. She never had time. She had to concentrate to try to find the answer to this conundrum. She loved riddles, but not under these circumstances. In this case, of course, she did not like it at all. She was making an effort to think about who would be the ones who could introduce themselves to someone who was unable to see one of them. It could be anything or anyone, anywhere and anytime. She closed her eyes for a moment, and opened them immediately, fearing that she would not be able to follow the girl's progress towards the bush. She had already travelled half the distance.

But Nsona could not really concentrate. She rather had in mind the images of her journey than any idea of a solution. She let her memories slip through while she was still looking at the young girl who had just walked around the bush to return to her starting point. It seemed to her that she was coming back very quickly, with a fluid, slow, steady and rather agonizing gait. She seemed to slip, as if pushed by an invisible hand. Perhaps she would become a neighbor of hers in the middle of these trees. Why not become friends? Obviously she was also doomed to wander in these places. She continued to watch her approach without any further reaction, as if she was no longer seeing her. The voice made her gather her minds again.

"So, I am listening to you."

She looked for the young girl. She was gone. And then everything lit up in her mind.

"The wind?" she says softly.

There was a silence. She waited a few more moments. She was looking around as if she expected to see someone or something that would prevail. But nothing happened. Only a groan caught her attention.

She saw Tembo struggling to get up, holding his head. He looked up and looked around.

"Quickly, you have to leave," he said, staggering. "Do not hang around here."

Then he pestered.

"This is what happens when one takes your world's appearance. All defects are included! I cannot wait to recover my own; it will at least be that benefic! Obviously you are not hurt, I am reassured."

Was it necessary to tell him what had just happened? Was it useful? Obviously the way was free again. They had just passed a new hurdle. How many were there left? Would Tembo be able to get her to the right place? She realized that it was not only up to him, but also to herself. Should she not rather say that it depended mostly on herself?

They made their way through the trunks and branches that still allowed a passage and resumed their trip. As they moved forward, Nsona noticed a slight change in Tembo. He suddenly seemed older than before. Was it still a consequence of fatigue coupled with darkness or was it real? The wind that began to blow again among the trees drew her from her reflections. The faster they went, the stronger he seemed to blow. Were other trees still going to fall in their path? And should she again answer a new riddle?

She might not always be inspired as she had been before.

"We must accelerate further," Tembo shouted in the wind, which continued to blow in increasingly violent gusts.

His voice seemed to have changed. It was no longer the soft, youthful voice she had known until then. But he was ahead of her, so she could not see what she imagined. She expected anything. After all she had been through, the impossible could be conceivable. This would explain many things and prove that even in the other world ex-humans remain very human. Feelings do not seem to change.

The edge of the forest of the wanderers finally began to appear. They continued at the same pace until they emerged in the sparse bushes and savannah that separated them from the next forest which was the last one before reaching Nzila Kumi. They left the forest without further trouble. In this area much more open to the sky, Nsona felt less oppressed. The places were actually more airy and permitted to see much further than in the forest. What would happen once they would get to the next one? But Tembo had taken a track that varied from the one they had followed when they had come. They were moving away from the forest they would have had to cross. Nsona saw it in the distance.

"Where are you taking me this time?" she asked him.

"There is less and less time. I am going to bring you closer to entering your world. There is no need to go down the same path. Especially since we are certainly expected there."

This time, Nsona was sure. Tembo's voice had completely changed. It was the voice of a mature man, a middle-aged man. But she still could not see his face. He continued to advance in front of her without even turning his head back, as if he wanted to conceal it. Suddenly the ground slipped away from their eyes. There was a kind of ravine in front of them. It was a dry riverbed. Tembo seemed to know what he was doing. He began to go along it without slowing down. They reached a small sandy slope that descended to the bottom of the ravine. There was another slope on the other side, which would allow to go up on the other side after crossing. It was a few hundred steps away. Tembo had slowed down as he descended the slope. As he arrived halfway, he stopped his horse and beckoned Nsona to do the same. He listened for a moment. Then he suddenly galloped his mount.

"Let us hurry up!"he yelled.

Without questioning, she followed him pushing both her mounts to the maximum. It was then that a rumble sounded. She looked up and searched around to try to understand what it was and above all where it came from. But she saw nothing. As for Tembo, he expressed no surprise. It was as if he knew this was going to happen. That is why he had asked Nsona to hurry. He was accelerating again, distancing Nsona more and more. Then, suddenly realizing her delay, he slowed down and let her join him. And as he grabbed her to pick her up on his mount, she saw a face with graying hair and beard. She was frightened, but she had no way to escape. In any case, she understood that he was doing what was necessary to save her when she saw that the rumble was even closer and she realized what it was. He accelerated his horse while the other two, harnessed together, lost ground again. A little further on, those who were carrying Nsona's belongings were making great efforts to keep pace. They were moving fast, but the water was coming even faster and the ground was sandy. They had to get out quickly. Water vapors were already coming at them, mixed with a huge cloud of dust. Already, Nsona could not see anything any more. She just felt carried away like a straw in Tembo's arm. The dust was starting to sting her eyes. She closed them.

She reopened them a few moments later. She saw the cloud of dust and water roll away. The streams gradually filled the bed. Very quickly, everything calmed down. There was no trace of the horses that had stayed behind. Tembo had just had time to move her own out of reach of the liquid fury that had just passed.

"They must really blame you for going so far as to trigger the elements! I did not really realize it. But paradoxically, if they are at that spot, it is because they feel a little helpless."

He turned to her.

"You must have close-knit ancestors who have effectively advocated your case. But let us remain vigilant."

"What would have been your reward?"

He took off his hood. She clearly saw a face far more marked by life than the one she had known until then. Tembo had undergone decades of aging in a few hours.

"I had the promise to have my youth back forever if I succeeded in my mission. Instead, I am going to be a wandering old man again. That is why we have to move fast. I shall soon no longer have the strength of a young man. Let us go!"

He put Nsona on the only mount they had left. He began to run, dragging the animal with him. Despite the advanced age he was beginning to display, he was still able to move much faster than a human of the same age could. How much time did he have left? If he lost his strength before she joined her world, what would happen to her if she were again on her own? She preferred not to think about it. There had been so much unforeseen that she was mentally preparing for everything. She was even convinced that she would finish the journey alone. This seemed increasingly evident to her as she noticed that Tembo's pace was slowing down. He ran through the bushes, zigzagging most of the time. There was no real path to be followed. However, Nsona could see he was going straight ahead. He was following a direction that would bring her home as soon as possible. She simply hoped that he would lead her as close as possible to her ordinary daily life.

*

Tembo stopped running gradually, but fairly quickly. He slowly collapsed as the horse came to stand near his body.

Nsona stayed for a moment with surprise and anguish. The moment she feared so much had arrived. She pulled herself together and rushed to the ground to see if he was still alive. She felt a shiver run down her spine despite herself. She looked mechanically around, as if to get help. But she knew she had nothing to look forward to. There was nothing left under the hooded cape that Tembo had worn moments earlier. He had simply vanished. What could she do?

She made her decision very quickly. She would continue straight in the same direction Tembo had followed. That would surely take her where she wanted to go. She got back on the horse and tried to move it forward. It did not move. She tried for a moment before realizing that she had no authority over the animal. Tembo's presence was apparently the element that made him obey. The animal was from here, he obeyed only the beings who resided there. She reluctantly set foot on the ground, looking far ahead. The bushes stretched as far as the eye could see. The sky was clearer than it had been since the morning. It was supposed to be a little over the middle of the day. She bravely set off trying to imitate the way that Tembo was following before he disappeared. She was circling the bushes, but tried to keep the same course.

She had been walking for a very long time. The landscape did not change. Hunger was pulling her stomach but she kept moving, hoping for a sign or clue to know where she was. But nothing was happening. She could not see anything. She went back on her footsteps, thinking that she had certainly missed a path somewhere, a construction or something else. But she still could not see anything. She eventually turned in circles until she was exhausted. She sat on a clod of earth and began to think.

How had she get to this point? If she made it, would she learn the lesson? Who could she tell the whole story? How could she explain coming back home alone when she had married and was supposed to be far from home living with her husband? Could she find a plausible explanation? Would people not say that even after saying "yes" she was still able to say "no"? She smiled.

She decided to get back on track no matter what. But once she was up, she did not know where to go. She had to face the fact: she was lost. She sat down against a bush that had a trunk strong enough to support her. She had to rest a little. She closed her eyes and without realizing it she fell asleep.

13

The voice that was speaking to her seemed to be in her head. It gently pulled her out of her torpor. She did not understand what it was saying to her. She then took a deep breath and eventually opened her eyes. In front of her stood an old but still strong looking man. He was wearing a large but black tunic with the inevitable hood. He did not look very friendly, but Nsona was happy to finally see someone. Had she finally arrived?

"Where am I?" she asked.

The old man looked at her without any emotion.

"Who are you?"

The question sounded like an alarm in the young woman's head. She had an old man in front of her, but the voice was a voice she had already heard and which had already asked her the same question. An indefinable voice, neither feminine nor masculine. Why appear to her this time? And if it was the same interlocutor she had already had, why was he asking the same question? She had a bad feeling.

"Is my time up?" she asked.

The old man kept staring at her.

"Who are you?" he insisted, without giving up a certain calm.

She introduced herself, then quoted her parents.

"Who brought you here? You could not have come here alone."

"It is Tembo, my husband. But he no longer is. He should never have been."

The old man stepped back and looked at her with incomprehension.

"What do you mean by that? Were you forced to marry him?"

"No, I..."

"Did you make that choice on your own?"

"Yes, but..."

"So, what happened?"

The young woman thought for a moment.

"He was not from my world, this union was doomed to failure. In addition he had other ambitions than marriage."

"He was not from your world? So why did you choose him?"

"I did not know he was not."

"You did not know that? Did you not know him? Had you never met him or had your parents?"

Nsona sighed.

"No," she said in a barely audible breath.

The old man raised his arm and pointed away.

"That is where you have to go."

She got up.

"Thank you."

"Do not thank me. You do not know what is coming up and particularly whether you are ever going to get back home.

"Thank you all the same."

She set off as the old man stood still and watched her move away. She turned around two or three times, and saw that he was still there, as if he wanted to make sure she was going in the right direction. The sky was getting brighter and brighter. But she finally was so far away that she no longer saw him. She was convinced that if she had gone the wrong way he would have intervened. Something from him seemed familiar to her. Who was he?

*

She arrived before a small wood whose trees were motionless. Yet she could feel the wind blowing. But not a leaf, not a branch reacted to this movement of air. Looking around, she realized that the surrounding bushes were lulled by this light breeze that was heading towards the trees without having the same effect. It was as if there was a border between the two zones.

She heard a sneer. She turned around.

"So you managed to get here! I should congratulate you! But I do not want to do so!"

She had just before her the old woman who had sneered when the first riddle had been submitted to her. The one who had yelled angrily when she had given the correct answer. This time, she was alone.

"What do you want from me?" Nsona yelled.

"Oooh! You still think it is just about you! But, I too have my problems. Tembo failed, but I am more subtle than he is. My mission is to bring you back if he does not. In any case, you must not leave. Obviously he has run out of time. So it is up to me now."

Nsona tried to escape, but she could not get very far. The old woman was very quickly in her way to stop her. She turned around, with no more result. She was tired and just could not take it anymore. Both physically and mentally. She stopped and decided to face her, as well as her own destiny.

"In order to succeed-and I will succeed-I have only one thing to ask you. You have already escaped from me twice. But you will not get away from me for a third time. The questions you were asked were far too easy. And you are a smart girl; that is why you got away with it. You also got away with it because you learned a lot from your journey here. It always pleases the ancestors and God when one learns of his mistakes, but I have no cure. I have a mission and I will accomplish it.

"What will be your benefit to bring me back to those who want to hurt me? Do you also hope to regain your youth?"

"Never mind. You would not understand. What I can tell you is that my only weapon is intellectual. But the consequences of failure will be for you physical."

Nsona sat on the ground and waited.

"Ah, I still see this as proof of your intelligence. You had rather preserve your strength to think."

"Stop the chatter! Ask me your question and let us be done with it!"

The old woman laughed again. She moved closer to Nsona.

"Ask my question?"

She sneered again.

"You have got it all wrong. I am not going to ask you any question, I am just going to ask you to say something."

She laughed again before getting quiet and stare at her.

"You tell me a sentence: if it is true I will take you back to the city of ancestors. If it is false, I will turn you into one of these bushes that surround you."

She chuckled loudly.

Nsona was exhausted. She was tired of struggling. She no longer had the desire or the strength to. She bowed her head to the ground and then collapsed, uttering her last will.

"You will take me to the city of ancestors." she sighed feebly.

*

A few days earlier, after his visit to Tembo's so-called family, pa Ebata had fallen seriously ill. He had come back and said that he had heard his friend's voice in the large house but then he did not really know what had happened. He had just remembered that he had entered and then he had woken up sitting in a seat in front of the entrance. There had been no one there, so he had just gone back home. He had been unable to say more. He had suddenly lost his voice and begun to suffer from a high fever. Despite the interventions of several healers, his condition had continued to worsen and he had died in barely bearable suffering. Pa Sadisa had been so shocked.

He had then learned of Lukuayi's disease, similar to that suffered by his younger brother. Her daughter's best friend had just had time to say that she had been visiting Tembo's family before she too lost her voice. He then made the connection with the house and concluded that something was going on there. But how could he prove anything? There could only be suspicion. Everyone thought that there was indeed a connection, but it would be difficult to deal with occult forces. It was better to avoid them as much as possible. So he did not seek to hold a supposed family accountable. Instead, he simply decided to set out to go at all costs to find his daughter, whom he now knew was in danger and that the son-in-law who had seemed so ideal was not so ideal.

He had therefore very quickly left Mbanza Miongo to go Mbuila in the hope of catching up with the young spouses before they arrived at their destination because he felt that otherwise the situation would be very difficult. He was accompanied by two of his younger brothers. For such a case, there was no question of him going alone. He had made some sacrifices in selling goods to get the best mounts possible. But at each of the places he knew had been his daughter's crossing points, what he had learnt had surprised him. They had always been way ahead of them. As they progressed, the gap between the young spouses' passage and theirs grew. So that when they had arrived at Nzila Kumi they had accumulated three long days of delay despite the steady pace they had imposed on their horses.

Pa Sadisa was still angry with himself for having ignored the advice of his late wife on Nsona's marriage. None of this would have happened. But how could he have known? Of course he could not have, but it would have been enough for him to honor the memory of ma Kimani by imposing her will on all, including Nsona. Would it only have been understood? The prospect of receiving gifts from the groom could sometimes make some people forget the meaning of reality.

His two companions and himself had spent the night in Nzila Kumi and they had left at dawn. The whole community knew they were leaving for Mbuila. They had spent so much time asking about the passage of their daughter's convoy and the direction to take that they had made a great name. The news had run through all the alleys that the father of the daughter of the impressive convoy that had passed a few days earlier was after her. So they had been told the way to Songo. Once he would get there, he would find out how to go to Mbuila. This route led straight to Songo and there was no other inhabited place before arriving. They were told that it took two long days of walking before reaching their destination. They had walked for a long time in an area covered with green bushes very pleasant to look at which almost made them forget the fundamental reason why they were in the area. What would they do once they would get there if they did not catch up with Nsona before she herself had arrived? For, if he was now sure of one thing, it was that they would not leave without her. He would not leave his daughter in the hands of this stranger who had been able to trick them so easily. But the consequences were great. Some of them were irreversible. There would undoubtedly also be the problem of the dowry to be repaid. But each thing in its time. He wanted his daughter back first.

*

Day 11

There were not many people on the ride. But those they met were not very talkative. In any case, no one had come across or heard of anyone who looked like the ones they described to them. They found it increasingly strange. It was not possible to go down this road without meeting all those who did the same. So what had happened? Had they gone so far ahead that those who came the other way had not even seen them?

They reached a small but dense undergrowth through which their road passed. There was obviously an unusual effervescence. They approached to see what was going on. When they got closer, they observed the scene. A group of people appeared to be stalking an animal that had taken refuge in the thicket among the trees. Some were running here and there.

"There!" a man shouted. "There! Right behind that bush over there!"

He beckoned to another who was further away.

"Be careful! It might try to get out on your side!"

"Do not worry," he replied. "I shall not give it a chance!"

He was wielding a long stick above his head.

Pa Sadisa drew closer and jumped off his horse, ready to help the group of men who were getting excited. Further aside, a few women watched with cries of encouragement but also of amazement.

"What is this animal that you are trying to neutralize?" he asked, taking a stick in his hand while his companions did the same.

"An animal?" one of the men replied with a loud laugh. "You have got it wrong! There! There! It is going a little deeper in the middle of the trees!"

"But what is it then?" pa Sadisa insisted.

"A bad genius!!" cried another man." Maybe that is all it is!"

"A bad genius? But how do you know?"

"How do we know? What else can it be? She wandered along the side of the road on her own and scruffy. What do you believe it can be? What would a single woman do here without even a piece of luggage?! In a white robe?!"

Pa Sadisa looked at his cadets. A bad genius with the form of a woman? It would be the first time they would see one.

"But if she is a bad genius," he said, "why is she hiding? She should be able to disappear, right?"

"She is weak! That is why!"

Pa Sadisa approached his cadets.

"Let us join them." he whispered to them. "This poor woman certainly needs help. Let us pretend that we also want her loss, but we shall encourage her flight as soon as a chance arises. The sooner we do that, the sooner we shall resume our way."

They joined the other groups that surrounded the undergrowth. They decided to enter a little deeper to have a better chance of intercepting the woman.

"Do you see anything?" a man shouted at them.

"No!" pa Sadisa replied. "She must be on your side or on the opposite flank!"

He decided to try a trick to attract the woman. He did not want to seem to be someone who did not believe in the supernatural, but he wanted to make the woman understand that she had a chance to get away with it if she came to him.

"Do you know what, folks?"

He continued to advance with his companions. A man echoed him.

"What is going on? Do you see her?"

Pa Sadisa kept peering at the bushes, exchanging complicit glances with his brothers.

"No, it is not about that! I do not think she is a bad genius! Tired or not tired, a genius does not hide in the middle of the trees or in the bushes! What do you think?"

There was no immediate response. He continued to move forward, focusing more on the response to him rather than on his environment. Then a voice sounded.

"So wait a little while for her to take you in her arms and cast a spell on you or dust you down!!"

No sooner had the sentence finished than pa Sadisa saw a shadow appear and throw itself upon him before he could react. In shock, he fell backwards.

"Oh,.. Papa! Papa! You came to get me! Oh, thank God!"

Pa Sadisa and his companions were surprised by the woman's appearance, but knew immediately who she was.

"Nsona!" one of the cadets said. "Is that you, Nsona?"

"Who else do you think it can be?"

"Uh, a bad genius?"

"I know you have always enjoyed joking, but this is not a moment to..."

She laughed and threw herself into the arms of each of them. pa Sadisa had regained his spirits.

"Nsona, my daughter! Let me look at you."

He held her by the shoulders and examined her from tip to toe.

"Are you okay?"

"I am as well as I can be, papa."

She looked at them in turn.

"What are you doing here?"

"This is no time for questions," one of the cadets said. "We have to get out of here. Quick, the horses!"

They rushed out of the undergrowth to run towards their mounts. But the women raised the alarm.

"She is out here! There she is! They are with her!"

Nsona stopped briefly.

"Maybe we should explain it to them!"

Her father took her by the arm and dragged her.

"I doubt they understand or even listen to us. They are too excited!"

They reached their mounts and galloped away as the first men approached them. They galloped without stopping, barely letting their mounts blow, until they reached the crossroads with the ten routes. Nsona recognized the place.

"Are not there eleven lanes that meet here?"

One of her uncles looked at her and answered her laconically.

"It seems to me that this place gave its name to the town of Nzila Kumi, right? So there are only ten ways. Logical, do you not think?"

He could not imagine what was going on in the young woman's mind. They stopped briefly at Nzila Kumi to change her clothes, which were actually scruffy and to get a mount for her. Then they headed back for Mbanza Miongo.

14

About ten days later, the quartet arrived at Mbanza Miongo. They arrived at night. This prevented Nsona from suffering the questionings of onlookers and answering the inevitable questions of each about this premature return. She was not prepared for it yet. She had to start by getting her head in order before facing the outside, after having faced her own family. She had explained to her father that there was no need to worry about having to pay back the dowry, but that it was better to get rid of what was left of it given its occult origin. It was better not to take any chances.

Fortunately for Nsona, her father had believed her. Given what he also knew on his side, he had every reason to do so. On the way back, she had told him about her journey from the start until her meeting with pa Ebata. If he had not been there, she was convinced that she would probably never have come back.

"I am sure that somehow he sacrificed his life for mine. I am sure he made a deliberate choice."

Pa Sadisa felt the guilt that was eating away his daughter. He tried to reassure her.

"Nsona, if that is what you think, then also tell yourself that he made a choice. And this choice he made out of love, believe me. He certainly found himself in a situation where he felt he had to do it. So the best way to pay tribute to him would be to thank him and not to regret his passing or to feel guilty."

The young woman would get used to it, but it would take time. She had spoken of pa Sadisa, but she had been unable to tell her father that she had also seen her best friend, Lukuayi, with her baby in her arms. The guilt was too strong and the pain indescribable. Strangely, she was not surprised to learn that she was still alive. She was still seriously ill, but still alive. To her, that was all that mattered.

She was now going to do her best to keep her alive. In eleven days, she had experienced an incredible event that had showed her that anything was possible. She knew that life did not stop at their existence alone. She knew that the ancestors were listening to their descendants and that they were simply waiting for them to ask for help to intercede in turn with God, and that they would act with the grace of God.

She also knew that no one would believe what she had experienced, even though popular belief was full of legends that presented such adventures. But could she keep such a weight to herself? Could she ever have a confidante to talk to? She was convinced that she would be considered to have lost her mind. Her father believed her and he was sincere. But she could not drag him into such a situation. He, too, would face charges of insanity.

What a paradox. A people so quick to believe in the supernatural, so quick to see evil spirits at the first opportunity and so quick to deny them as soon as confirmation of their existence occurred. But she could not remain neutral in her life with such great knowledge in her possession. Beyond her personal case, she was convinced that what she had experienced had not been in vain. She had to share it with as many people as she could. She would find out how.

*

A few months later, Nsona was in the family yard of her best friend Lukuayi. She was holding the baby who had just come to birth a few days earlier. She was the happiest of all the people who were present. But she alone knew why. Unfortunately, she could not share it with anyone. Not even with Lukuayi.

When she had come out of the coma and recovered, she had simply asked her:

"Come on! What are you doing here? Should you not be in Mbuila? You cannot have come back so fast, have you?"

She had simply answered her in a sobbing but unpretentiously happy voice.

"Do not worry about it. I am here and I am not leaving any more."

"You are not going back?!" she had asked with big eyes. " What about your husband? Who will take care of him?"

"Do not worry, it was a mistake that is now far behind us."

"A mistake? And this dowry worthy of a princess, which you are by the way, a mistake too? How do we deal with it all, Nsona?!"

"Do not worry," she had gently reassured her. "I am telling you, everything is in order."

Lukuayi had looked at her calmly.

" You seem so confident. Then I shall believe you."

They had then embraced with happiness.

Before that day, Nsona had often made the journey between Mbanza Miongo and Bouaki. She would come to her friend's bedside to pray for her recovery. Some imagined it was a miracle that she had fully recovered, but particularly as she had not lost her baby. But Nsona knew it was not. She had prayed hard and with great faith. She knew that she would be heard and that her request would be effectively relayed to the almighty. So she was not surprised to see her recover as if nothing had happened. She had asked that her friend be able to come back; she knew it was possible, and she had been granted.

The solution had then became obvious to her. She would become a prayer woman. She would pray at the request of those who had trouble doing it on their own. She would pray for those who could not do it themselves. She would pray for those who needed it. It would be a way for her to share her secret, without sharing it. She had then begun to pray for others. At first there had been sarcasm. But in the face of the growing satisfaction of those who appealed to her, she was taken more and more seriously. She prayed only for positive requests, and she very often achieved positive results. There were no more marriage proposals for her because it was rumored that she had now become the one who conversed with the ancestors. She did not converse with them; she just talked to them. She still remembered one of the phrases that had been said to her: "We do not die, we just go to sleep."

Lukuayi came out of the house and walked up to her friend.

"So how are you doing with the kid?"

"He is looking at me laughing."

"It is strange, you know. There are times, when he looks at you, I feel like he recognizes you for having seen you somewhere."

"Oh yes? Where?"

"Well,... I do not know."

Nsona began to sing a lullaby to the child.

"My child, mama is here
  And you have your life ahead of you
  My child, mama is here.
  And the world is all yours
  My child, mama is here.
  Close to you, do not worry
  My child, mama is here.
  All your life, she will be."

****

May 2020

9 782956 627746